Autumn Sand

Bonded

A Twisted Hearts Love Story

Bonded: A Twisted Hearts Love Story

Copyright © Autumn Sand 2017

eBook ISBN 978-0-9967954-7-0

Library of Congress Control Number 2017942183

Cover design by Pixel Mischief

Edited by All About The Edits

Proofread and Formatted by The Last Step Proofreading

Disclaimer

Dear Reader,

      As the author of this book, I want to warn readers that there is child abuse in the subject matter. Though I do not necessarily go into the details of the abuse, it is implied. I do not in any way condone these acts nor do I glamorize them. As usual, I am using my books to shed more light on a vicious and heinous act and hopefully show a way to heal.

Thank you,

Autumn Sand

Twisted Hearts Love Stories

Everyone has a story to tell either through written words or through other means. We each had things that have had a profound effect on us in some way, and it has changed the course of our life. That is what the Twisted Hearts Love Stories represent. Hope and lessons learned all the while finding love and happiness. Most importantly knowing it does not make you weak when you learn to depend on another to help you.

This series is also meant to be a fast-paced thrill ride while touching on hard subjects.

This is from one hopeful soul to another, read this if you dare.

Autumn

Prologue

No Church In The Wild ~ Jay-Z & Kanye West

10 Years Ago

Oh, my God.

If he catches me, I know he'll kill me. Ignoring my cramped muscles, I pump my legs harder, trying not to run into one of the many tree branches that are determined to slow me down. The crackling sound of dead leaves beneath my feet threaten to give away my location as I zig-zag through the forest. Turning my head, I squint my eyes as I stare into the darkness hoping not to see him. A sharp pain hits my toe as I stumble across a rock. Reaching out into the night, grasping at nothing but air, I desperately try to steady my balance. I don't see any sign of him behind me, but my pace doesn't slow. I run harder and faster, trying not to concentrate on the burning sensation in my lungs.

"MARIE! When I catch you this time, you fucking bitch, you're *dead*. You hear me?"

I slam myself against a nearby tree and steal another glance behind. My breathing is labored as I take huge gulps of air into my lungs. He has to be close if I can hear him that clearly. Holding my hands over my mouth, I try not to let the cry of fear escape. *Mustn't let out a sound or else.* My body trembles as I steady myself on the tree, as I close my eyes and try to focus. *RUN. Damn it, Marie. Just keep running.*

I run deeper into the forest, realizing I've lost my direction. I stop, turning around and around frantically, hoping to see a landmark so I can gather my bearings. In the densely-covered forest, the moonlight is barely showing. To make matters worse, a few days ago, I saw a news report about black bears attacking hikers in the area. I'm not sure what I fear most: the possibility of spotting a bear...or him. I swallow the mixture saliva and blood, and nausea hits me in waves. The blood is a result of the face pounding he gave me just a few hours ago.

What is that up ahead? Is that a clearing? So close, yet so far away. Pushing through the endless branches, I approach the clearing after what feels like an eternity. Dropping to my knees, in case he isn't too far behind me, I try to stay hidden behind the shrubbery. I know this place. This is the back road that goes towards the Kayuta Lake campgrounds. There is a convenience store a few yards up the road that should still be open since it's camping season. With my trembling hand, I wipe away the beads of sweat from my upper lip. I remain crouched as I push through the shrubs and onto the road, where the moonlight shines through like a beacon. With one more glance behind me, I try to steel my emotions, before I break out into a full-on run in the direction of the convenience store.

I see the fuel pumps in front of the store first, and I let out a sob. Almost there. *It's now or never Marie, just keep moving forward.* As if I were running towards the finish line in the race of my life, I lunge for the door handle.

Locked.

NO, NO, NO. This can't be happening. I pound on the glass door, hoping to catch Nate's attention, who is apparently napping at the front counter. He shifts his baseball cap from covering his face and looks up. Rubbing his eyes with the back of his hands, he squints to see who is at the door, and I wave frantically at him. Stretching on the back end of a yawn, he stands and walks towards the door. I look behind me to make sure that *he* isn't close.

Turning back to the door, I shake the handle and bang again, in hopes that it will speed up the slow clerk. He finally reaches the door and opens it, peeking his head out. "What's the rush for, Marie? You need gas?" he asks, still yawning and stretching.

"No, I need a telephone," I cry.

"A telephone?" The lines of his mouth turn downward, and he takes in my appearance. "Marie, what happened to you?"

Grabbing his biceps, I squeeze. "I need to call the police. Do you understand?" I look behind me to see if I've been found. Turning back to Nate, "I need the cops before he finds me." My voice cracks as panic – real, absolute, terrifying fear - settles in. I let go of him and hold myself, hoping to stop the trembling.

Lifting up his baseball cap, he scratches the top of his head. "Before *who* finds you?"

Irritated, I push past him and walk inside the store, Nate following behind me. The stench of mildew hits my nose, and I swallow hard to keep from vomiting. "Lock the door," I yell to him as I walk behind the counter and locate the phone. I press the buttons that I've longed to press. 9-1-1.

The rush of adrenaline that was pushing me forward leaves my body so quickly the room spins out of control. The operator comes on the line, and before I can get my words out, I collapse.

Chapter 1

<u>Sprinkle Me ~ E-40 feat. Suga-T</u>

Magnum

Present Day

It's been a long day at Pulse X, with the overseeing of hiring staff for Tony Delaney's new club in Amsterdam. The club is set for a grand opening in a month. Usually, Tony would have sent Tick, but since he and Cyma are expecting their first baby together, Manny and me came in his place. I can't complain; hell, who *would* complain about coming to the city of the Red Light District? Not me, that's for damn sure.

I stand up to stretch my legs. The process has taken hours, and while interviewing the hostesses has been fun, it's unbelievable what some of these women would do to get hired. And why not? Pulse X is going to be the hottest thing to hit Europe in a long time. Pulse X, unlike Pulse in the States, will be edgier...with a lot of sex. Nope, not selling actual ass, but the image of sex. Our goal is to make these people want it so bad that whoever leaves here will be on their way home to fuck, or fucking on their way out the door.

"That was the last interview of the day, I think," Manny says, as he lights up his cigarette.

I flex my shoulders to relax my tense muscles. A big guy like me, who is usually active, is not used to sitting behind a desk for long periods of time. "Yeah, believe so." I sit back down and throw my feet on top of the desk, leaning back in the chair. "Call it a day?"

"Fuck yeah. Don't know how Tick and Tony do this shit on a regular basis." Manny blows out a puff of smoke.

I shrug, leaning forward to pick up the last job application. "S'not so bad."

"My man, nothing is so bad as 'not so bad'."

I let out a loud guffaw.

He sits up and straightens his suit jacket. "Might be hooking up with one or two of them tonight." A wide smile spreads across his face as he winks.

"Club ain't even open and you already fucking the help?" I stretch again and yawn.

"Let's just say I'm breaking them in," he admits with a laugh, before throwing his head back to blow smoke rings into the air.

Tick and Manny have each gone through their fair share of the hostesses at Pulse back in the states. Now that Tick is off the market, Manny seems to be picking up the slack.

I laugh at him and shake my head. This guy will never change. With nothing left to take care of today, I'm not sure why I'm still hanging around. *Time to go.*

"I'll check you later." I stand quickly and give him a pound.

"You know how to find me."

Yeah, up some woman's pussy is usually the first place to check. I exit the office, laughing again at his previous comments. Some of the newly hired staff say goodnight to me as I pass by them. Can't remember their names yet. I do remember their measurements, but refrain from calling them by numbers, simply nodding at them as I leave. Outside in Leidseplein Square, I walk the short distance to my hotel. Thinking about buying a place out here, since it seems I might be spending more time in Amsterdam. Once we hire a manager to oversee the day to day activities, I expect to be out here every couple of months, and it would be nice to have a place to call home when I do. But my hotel is comfortable, and I do have a suite that is like a mini apartment, so I can't really complain.

I walk inside the hotel lobby, and am greeted by some of the staff. I say my hellos to each by name. The elevator ride to my floor is quick and uneventful as I ignore a woman who's making a pass at me. She looks hot with her large breasts - probably fake - and nice shaped legs, but I don't bother to give her a real glance. I've certain tastes, and she doesn't fit my requirements. Most women are turned on by my body art and piercings. They think it makes me dark, mysterious, and perhaps dangerous. Trust me, I'm all they think I am, and have the stories to prove it.

Once inside my suite, I pour myself a scotch. Popping an ice cube in my mouth, I chew on it as the cube hits my tongue ring. I lay back on my sofa and try to figure out what am I doing for the rest of the night, debating if I should call Tick and give him an update, or find some trouble to get into. The bright red numbers on the digital clock tell me it's too early in the States to call him. Don't want to wake Cyma. A yawn escapes my mouth, and I fight sleep, which has always been an enemy of mine. Too many memories I don't want to remember always seem to find their way into my dreams. The perfect remedy for that is not to sleep, so I don't. I catch naps mostly, and on the rare occasion my body gives in to my nemesis, I fall into a sleeplike coma for a day or two.

Instead, I head to the bathroom and splash some cold water on my face. Looking into the mirror, my eyes are red-rimmed, and I know I need some rest. *A cold shower is what I need to wake me up.* I turn on the cold spray and undress, removing my various rings with skulls and spikes. I take a quick shower and get dressed in dark blue jeans and a black t-shirt. I think I just figured out what I will be doing for the night. Back outside in Leidseplein Square, I get into a waiting cab and give him the address of my destination and, twenty minutes later, we pull up. I pay him and get out, looking up at the window of the building. The curtain is open, but I don't see her. A red light becomes my beacon as I walk to the door and before I can knock, she opens it.

Standing in front of me with nothing but a smile on her face, she loops a finger through my belt loop and pulls me into the room, the door slamming behind me.

"Ziet eruit als ik ga een goed neuken vanavond," she says to me. *Looks like I'm going to have a good fuck tonight.*

My cock pushes against my jeans to get to her, and I pull her against me, chest to chest. She cups my dick through my jeans, and a wide smile spreads across her face as she licks her lips hungrily.

"Rauw vanavond?" she concludes. *Rough tonight?* Taking my hand, she leads me into another room with a bed.

"Is er een andere manier?" I ask her in my limited Dutch. *Is there another way?* I know enough to get my dick sucked and to order a drink. English is not an issue in this country.

"You've been practicing?" she asks, as she walks over to a drawer that holds her play toys. Her every movement has me hypnotized. I debate if I should forego the toys, and just grab her and fuck her from behind, just this once.

"Enough." My eyes never leave her ass, and I watch as she holds up one item and then another. I take off my t-shirt and throw it on the floor before unzipping my jeans and releasing my quickly hardening dick.

She finds the items she's looking for and walks over to me. I take the nipple clamps and paddles from her, as she kneels down on the floor in front of me, her head hung low. Waiting for me.

The scene is set just the way I like it: ass up, face down.

Chapter 2
What's The 411? ~ Mary J. Blige feat.Grand Puba

Brenda

"I'm sorry, Mr. and Mrs. Wilson, but we couldn't save her." Dr. Cross relays the earth-shattering news to the now grieving parents.

I know I should stay in the room with the parents until the grief counselor arrives, but I can't. I just can't do it. I snatch my latex gloves off and throw them in the red wastebasket, pushing past the doctor, and leaving the room as quickly as possible, the mother's sobs pulling at my heart and pushing me up the hall. We fought hard for forty minutes, trying desperately to save Bella, but her little body couldn't take anymore. Didn't I become a nurse to save lives? I'll never understand, with all the modern-day medicine we have, when we still lose a child. *Fuck.* I hate it when I lose a patient. It's even harder when it's a child.

I walk past Lelia's former room that is now occupied by another sick child. Lelia is my best friend Cyma's daughter. Lelia was diagnosed with leukemia when she was two years old and would often be on this floor, and I was one of her nurses. That's how me and her mother met. If it wasn't for the bone marrow transplant from her father, Lelia might not be alive today.

"Rough night?" Kim, another nurse, asks me as I pour myself a cup of coffee in the break room.

"Yeah. Lost a patient," I say, as I stare at my cup of black coffee. Maybe if I look at it hard enough, it'll turn into vodka.

"Oh no. It never gets easy, does it?" she replies, shaking her head in sympathy. Her statement is something we all feel at one time or another. It doesn't get easy, and it's hard to look at a patient and not put the human aspect into it. As hard as you try not to get attached, it's still tough to watch a patient die.

"No, it doesn't, and the day that it does, then I know it's time for me to quit," I tell her as I plop into a seat beside her.

Dr. Cross walks in, pours a cup of joe, and takes a seat next to us.

I feel immediately guilty for running out of the room earlier. "I'm so sorry about that, Doc-"

"When it's just us, please call me Ray." He gives me a warm smile.

Doctor Raymond Cross is a dark-haired man with dark olive skin. All of the nurses, including myself, have had a crush on him at one time or another. We've had a semi-flirtatious work relationship, but honestly, I don't believe in shitting where I eat. So, I've cooled it down a bit, but he is still full steam ahead and not quite taking the hint.

I nod, "Sorry, Ray. It just got to me when we lost Bella. I promise it won't happen again." I lift my cup to take a sip of the sludge.

"It will happen again, and that is what I like about you. It's not just a job for you."

There is just something about the way he looks at me that is making me feel awkward, and I shift a little in my seat.

"Hey, some of us are going out after our shift. You should join us. It could cheer you up." I'm thankful for Kim's interruption.

I debate going out with them, but my energy left the moment Bella was pronounced dead. "I'll pass this time but thanks for the offer."

"You should go." Ray stares at me as if he is undressing me with his eyes.

Kim reaches across the table and touches my hand. "You really should come."

"I have just enough energy to finish my shift and go home. Next time, definitely count me as a yes." I stand and toss my half-touched coffee in the garbage so I can go back to my patients.

Disappointment settles on Ray's face, but he tries to hide it by bringing his cup of coffee to his lips.

"Sure thing. See you tomorrow." Kim smiles at me as I walk away.

"Day after. I'm off tomorrow," I tell her as I head back out on to the floor.

A few hours later, I'm walking down my block in Queens, juggling my groceries I picked up, courtesy of the twenty-four-hour bodega around the corner. Now I can sleep in tomorrow and not worry about food shopping. I really should look into having my groceries delivered. I often pick up extra shifts at the hospital to keep busy, and I find grocery shopping a chore I rather not do. I walk up the four steps to the door of my two-story house. Setting my groceries on the ground, I go through my purse in search of my house keys. I seem to lay my fingers on everything but my keys as I let out an exasperated breath. *UGH. Finally found them.* I push the key into the lock, and my door opens. *What the…?* I know I locked my door when I left this morning. Didn't I? I was in a rush and extremely tired but I would've remembered that.

I stare at the open door, afraid to step inside. "Good evening, Brenda," my neighbor calls out to me from behind. I turn around to see David walking his Rottweiler, Finster. The dog runs up the steps and stands on his hind legs as his two front paws rest on my thighs.

I bend to pat him. "Hey, Fin. That's a good boy." I use the tone of voice adults use when speaking to animals and children. I scratch behind his ear as he tries to lick my face.

"You spoil him," David chuckles as he climbs the steps.

I hug Fin to me and pat him on the back. "Oh, he just needs a hug from me."

"Down, Fin. Down boy," David says, and Fin ignores him as usual. He grumbles under his breath.

A few more pats later, Fin is happy and goes back to David. "Hey, would you mind walking inside with me? I seem to have forgotten to lock the door when I left for work."

"Sure, no problem. You did fly out of your house like a bat out of hell this morning." David is an artist and works out of his house, though most of his time seems to be spent staring out his window.

"Yeah, I woke up late. Pulled a double yesterday and was just exhausted when I woke up." David helps me with my bags, and we walk down the hall to the kitchen. Placing the bags on the marble counter top, I look around to see if anything looks out of order.

"I'll walk through the house with you, to be sure," David offers, as Fin runs around the house like it's his personal playground, barking up a storm.

"Thanks. Greatly appreciated." We walk out of the kitchen and into the living room. "Everything looks good in here. Let's check the upstairs." Fin beats us to the staircase and bounds up the steps, where he waits for us on the top landing. We check the guest rooms and bathroom, and finally my bedroom. I turn on the lights when we walk in.

"Anything out of place?" David asks, as Fin takes the opportunity to park himself on my expensive duvet. He tries to shoo Fin off, but the dog isn't having any of it as he stretches out and rests his chin on his paws.

"No, I think everything is okay." I sit down next to Fin and stroke his back absentmindedly.

"Come on, Fin. Get down now." Fin's response is to roll on his back, so I can rub his tummy.

"It's okay. Fin and I have an understanding." Fin barks and David rolls his eyes.

"I should get going. Gotta finish walking the mutt, ya know." He points his thumb at Fin, who is loving his belly rub so much his tongue is hanging out of his mouth.

"Thanks for walking through with me." I stand and follow David out of the bedroom with Fin walking behind us.

"Sure. That's what neighbors are for." He stops and looks at the painting he gave me some time ago that is hanging on my hall wall. "You kept it?"

I walk up behind him. "Of course I did. I told you I would hang it."

He turns to look at me and smiles. "That means a lot to me."

"Well it meant a lot to me when you gave it to me." I dip my chin.

We stay like this for a moment before he says, "I really need to get going."

I walk him downstairs and hold the front door open. Fin stops and looks at me and then David, as if he is confused who to follow. David pulls a snack out of his pocket and Fin's affections have officially been swayed. It's just like the saying goes; the way to a man's heart is through his stomach. Looks like Fin just proved that in spades.

"Goodnight, and thanks again," I say. David turns around and waves.

Back inside, I head to the kitchen to put my groceries away. Too tired to cook dinner, I grab a yogurt and eat that quickly. Besides, I'm not really that good of a cook. Give me Cup of Noodle soups any day. I walk around the first floor to make sure all doors are locked before heading upstairs. Showering quickly and changing into my sleep clothes hanging on my bathroom door, I walk into my bedroom, and the lights are out. I thought I turned them on when we came upstairs earlier. I must've instinctively turned them off when I walked David and Fin downstairs. But...weren't they on when I came up to take my shower? I shake my head. "Get it together, Brenda. You're losing it, girl." I flip the switch but it doesn't come on. "Silly Brenda. The lightbulb just blew. Stop being paranoid," I say out loud to myself, and go downstairs to get a new lightbulb.

Chapter 3

River ~ Leon Bridges

Magnum

Sitting at a crowded bar with Manny on a Friday night, we unwind. We finished all our interviews and have finally put together a team to work Pulse X. We also hired a manager, who will start his training under me tomorrow. So Manny and I decided to go out and celebrate. Tony is happy with the progress we have made, and now the only thing we have to do is worry about the opening in another month. Should be a breeze from here. Anaya, Tony's wife, put together an A-list of invitees, and it'll have some press coverage as well. The bar is cloudy with cigarette smoke, and Manny feels right at home.

"Man, I think I want to move here," Manny muses, as he stares at a woman in daisy dukes and high heels.

"Great place to visit, but I don't know about moving," I reply as I stare at the same woman. *Damn, her ass is tight.*

"What time you heading in tomorrow?"

I shrug. "Eh, not sure. Got the trainee coming in at one, so I guess sometime before then."

"Telling you now, I'm not coming in that early. Getting my dick sucked and plan on nursing a hangover." He lifts his glass in salute to me.

"Guess you earned it. Burn off some steam." In the back of my mind, I ponder if I should go and pay my friend a visit and my dick twitches at that thought. I reach into my pocket, pulling out a wad of cash to settle the tab.

"You out?"

"Yeah. You just reminded me of something I have to take care of." I neglect to say that the *something* is *someone*. We pound it out, and I hop in the first cab I see.

****

I can make this shot. I dribble the ball down the court and fake a left, jumping up for a slam dunk. Hands grab my ankle, and I am pulled down to the ground. Fuck, that shit fucking hurts! A sharp pain goes through my arm, and I close my eyes, trying not be a punk and cry in a stadium full of high school students. The crowd quiets down as my coach walks over to me.

Kneeling next to me, Coach Phillips asks, "You alright, son?"

I bite my bottom lip as the searing pain shoots up my arm. "Yeah. Give me a sec." I sit up with the help of my coach.

He hesitantly touches my arm and looks at me. "Looks like it is broken."

FUCK. FUCK. FUCK. If it's broken, then I'm out of the playoffs. My father is going to kill me. I look over to the bleachers where my father is sitting in his usual seat. His angry eyes stare at me, and I cringe. "Put me back in, Coach. I can play."

He shakes his head at me. "No way, son. It's the ER for you."

My father is approaching us, and I secretly want to hide behind my coach rather than suffer my father's wrath. "What's wrong?" he asks.

"Looks like his arm is broken. He needs to go the ER."

"Da fuck you say? There are scouts sitting out there. You can still play, can't you, Carl?"

"Yes. Yes, Sir. I can play with one arm, Sir." I was raised to call my father, Sir. He says it's respect.

"You see. Carl is okay. He can play." My father straightens his spine to his full six-foot four-inch height, towering over my coach, who stands at five-foot-eleven.

"Now, listen here. I'm the coach, and I say he can't play. He has to go to the ER." My father's eyes turn to slits because he is not used to anyone disagreeing with him. When he gives a direct order, people listen.

"He has a lot riding on this game. I didn't waste years and money getting him ready for this moment. He's going to be a pro one day. In order for him to get that, he needs to get into a Division One college." My father turns and points his fingers at the bleachers. "And those are Division One scouts. So I say he plays."

The referee comes over to us to see what the problem is. The crowd is getting antsy and starting to boo.

"Problem?" the referee asks.

"No problem. Carl is out. He broke his arm." Coach ignores my father's wishes.

The referee nods and walks away to talk to the other team's coach.

Seeing that he got outplayed, my father turns and walks towards the exit. I stay behind, unsure of what to do. Coach puts his hands on my shoulders and gives me a sympathetic look. "You okay?"

Tears threaten to fall down my cheeks, but if my father saw that, he would really give me something to cry about. I swallow back the tears and nod. "Yeah. Guess I'm out for the season."

Coach lowers his head and then looks at me. "Let's not jump to conclusions. Let the doc check you and we'll take it from there."

I grab on to any amount of hope that I can, and I smile weakly at him before turning towards the exit to follow my father.

Once outside, I see my dad already sitting in his car in the school parking lot, waiting for me. I take in a deep breath and let it out slowly to steady my nerves, then get inside the front passenger seat and close the door. Don't look at him. If you look at him, he might get angrier.

"Broken?"

I've heard about how farmers are so attuned to the weather that they can sniff the air and know if it is going to rain, snow, or even if there's a tornado coming their way. I take a deep inhale and sniff the air in the car, and I smell fear - my own. Fear of what's about to come.

"I guess." I don't look at him, wishing the car seat would open up and swallow me whole. A punch lands squarely on the side of my face and my head hits the window with a snap.

"I'll take you home first to teach you a lesson. You laid on that ground like a fucking girl. A son of mine, acting like a fucking pussy. You're an embarrassment to me. I'll teach you how to be a man yet."

Another punch is laid on me, but this time on my broken arm. A shot of pain goes through me. Don't cry, don't cry. It'll just make the beating worse if you cry. Be a man and don't cry.

****

"Magnum. Magnum, wake up." Hands are on the arm that was broken all those years ago, and I sit up in the bed with a start.

Instinctively, I rub my arm, feeling the pain as if it were yesterday. Fuck. I must've fallen asleep after fucking the shit out of her last night. I never fall asleep after a scene. I turn to look at her, and her brow is furrowed with worry.

"You alright?" she asks, her voice timid.

I shake the cobwebs out of my head before answering. "Yeah. Must've dozed off. Sorry about that."

She reaches her hand out to touch my cheek, and I flinch. She frowns and places her hand back on her lap. I want to reach for her, but that damn dream still has me out of sorts. I feel like an asshole; I'm just all kinds of fucked up, so I pull her into me for a quick peck on her lips. She smiles at that, and it relaxes her, but not me. My dream is still fresh in my mind, and I can't shake that feeling. My tongue moves around my mouth and finds the empty spot where a tooth used to be, courtesy of my father that day.

I stand quickly and grab my jeans, putting them on.

"You're leaving? I was happy that you stayed last night." She pouts at me. Our arrangement started out with me as a paying customer, but eventually, she stopped charging. She said she really likes fucking me because I always make sure she gets off. Her other clients don't extend that same courtesy.

"Yeah." I zip up my jeans and reach for my t-shirt. "Sorry about that. Got shit to do." She crawls across the bed to me, slow and seductive. Sitting up on her knees, she gives my nipple piercings a tug. I growl at her as my dick reacts. As I am about to lay her back on the bed and fuck her senseless, my cell rings. I inhale deeply and debate if I should answer it. Shit, it might be Tony or Tick.

I pull away from her, and she tries to pull me to her. "Have to take this call." I reach into my pants pocket and grab my cell. "Yeah?" I say, without looking at the caller id.

"CJ. It's Mom. You need to come home right away. Your father has had a heart attack."

Chapter 4
Stuck In The Middle With You ~ Stealers Wheel

Brenda

Even though Cyma is due to give birth any day now, we still don't miss girls' night. Only difference is, instead of being at a bar like we would've done normally before she was pregnant, we are sitting in her kitchen eating a pint of ice cream with Anaya.

"Hey, stop hogging all the chocolate syrup and give some to the pregnant lady," Cyma complains.

"If I can't have vodka when I'm around you, then I'm getting the chocolate syrup," I reply, while waving my spoon at her.

"I would love a chocolate martini," Anaya says, licking her lips.

"Some friends you two are. Stealing the food from my mouth. I'm eating for two. And all you want to talk about is chocolate martinis." She laughs and places her hand on her swollen stomach.

"Is the baby kicking?" I ask, getting a little giddy. I love to feel her stomach when the baby is active.

"Yes." She smiles brightly. "Want to feel?" She knows I do, but she also knows I'm being polite by waiting for her to ask.

I nod with a broad smile on my face. I stand and walk over to her, placing both hands on her stomach. The feeling of this little life making contact with my hands is emotional, and a tear falls down my cheek. "I'm in love with this baby already," I murmur.

"Well, you should. You're going to be the godmother." She smiles back at me.

"I can't wait," I say, clapping my hands together. "I already figured out ways to spoil the baby. And I'll be changing one of my guest rooms into a nursery."

"You're going overboard," she chides.

"I plan on doing as much babysitting duty as I can. I'm even going to cut back on all the overtime I usually do."

"You're going to be a great godmother," Anaya says to me while taking another spoonful of rocky road ice cream out of the container. She closes her eyes and licks her spoon clean. "Oh, my God, that is good."

"It is, right?" Cyma dips her spoon in, scraping the sides of the container.

I walk over and grab my spoon for another taste. "Better than sex," I muse.

They both look at me. "Oh no. Now *that* I won't say." Anaya laughs out loud.

"Agreed. That's how I got in this condition." Cyma points to her stomach with the now empty spoon.

Easy for them to say; they have hot men to go home to. I have my...oh yeah, my empty house. I'll take the ice cream as a substitute any day.

I shrug at them and dip in for another spoonful. "I don't have a sex life, so I guess I'll take your word for it."

"About that. You need to date," Cyma nudges.

"No time," I tell them. That is only partially true, though. Whenever a man gets too close, I usually cut it off, not wanting to have to explain things.

"There is always time." Anaya looks at me sympathetically.

"Not for me," I retort.

"What about Magnum?" Cyma asks, while reaching for her water bottle. "The two of you looked really into each other as I recall."

She's talking about the first time Magnum and I met. Cyma was just put out of her apartment by her landlord, and Magnum was keeping tabs on her as a favor for her now-husband, Tick. He was there that night, and we were definitely into each other. Or at least, I was into him. He drove me home, and I gave him my number. We went out once or twice, but then he abruptly stopped calling and never returned my phone calls. So, I guess, as they say, he just wasn't that into me.

"That ship sailed," I mumble.

"Magnum is such a pussycat," she says, while rubbing her stomach. "He is perfect for you."

"We went out, and even made out. But he stopped calling. Guess he didn't like me. I don't know. Sometimes I feel like a misfit." My shoulders slouch.

29

"Fine, then we'll just have to find you someone else," Anaya announces, holding up her finger in declaration.

"I'm fine. Don't worry about me. I'm too busy at work, and the baby will be here soon, so I really don't have the time for a relationship of any sort." Though, I wouldn't mind having a good fuck. Some mind-blowing sex really couldn't hurt. It really has been too long. David and I almost had sex a few months ago. That is, until I felt what he was working with and decided I really wasn't that desperate. I happen to be one of those women who take it personally when a man doesn't meet up to at least average. Unfortunately, David was way below that. I shudder at the thought of that night.

"I better get home. I left Tony with Xavier, and he is going through the 'terrible twos' phase." Anaya sighs out loud as she stands and walks over to first give Cyma a hug, and then me.

"I should go too. I have a lot of errands to run tomorrow." I stand and place my spoon in the sink, before leaning down to give Cyma a hug.

"Thanks for coming over," Cyma says, standing up and walking us to the front door. "Bren, make sure you call me to let me know you got home okay."

I smile at her and wave. Stepping outside, I walk over to my car and wave bye to Anaya, who is walking across Cyma's yard to get to her house.

My drive home is quick, thank goodness; traffic is light tonight. I go over my mental checklist of things I have to do tomorrow as I park my car and get out, chirping my alarm. The evening is nice out. A spring breeze whips through the air, and I can smell my neighbor's flowers that are in bloom. I close my eyes and enjoy the scent of spring, smiling as I walk up the steps to my front door and unlock it. Walking inside, I flip on the lights and lock the door behind me, humming a tune that I heard on the radio. I grab a soda from the kitchen and head into the living room to watch some ratchet television. As I walk towards my coffee table to grab the remote, the sound of glass crunches beneath my feet. *What the...?*

I look down and let out a bloodcurdling scream, dropping the soda I was carrying. The cold brown liquid splashes onto my legs and I jump back, more from fear of what lies on the floor than the soda. The can lay on its side, oozing out and onto the floor, mixing with the broken glass that came from my window and a dead rat, whose entrails are hanging out and tied to a rock. My adrenaline spikes and without a second to think, I run out of my front door and straight to David's house.

Bang. Bang. Bang.

I pound my fist on the door as tears fall down my cheeks in streams. I look behind me to make sure whatever maniac threw that in my window wasn't behind me. *Oh, please, oh please be home, David.*

BANG. BANG. BANG.

Fin barks at the door and scratches. Lights flicker on in the house, and I see David peek through his living room curtain. Realizing it is me, he yells out, "Be there in a sec."

He unlocks the door and opens it. Not bothering to wait for him to invite me in, I push past him and run inside his living

31

room. "Bren? What happened?" He comes over to me in nothing but his boxer shorts and holds me to him, stroking my back gently as I sob.

"Someone threw a dead rat into my living room," I cry into his shoulder. He holds me at arm's length to look at me.

"What did you say?"

"A dead rat, David. Someone threw a dead rat in my living room." I place my hands over my face, trying to keep it together.

"Stay right here." David goes to his hall closet, and I hear a rustling sound as if he is searching for something. I take a seat on his couch and Fin bounces around my legs, hoping to play. Moments later, he steps back into the living room with a baseball bat in hand. "I'm going to your house to take a look. You call the cops in the meantime."

"*No!* Don't leave me here."

He comes over and takes my chin in his hand.

"Don't worry. Fin is here to protect you." He turns and leaves.

Fin has jumped up on the couch and is trying to lick my face. I stand and go to the kitchen to use his house phone and call 9-1-1. Fifteen minutes later, two police officers show up, and David has already come back. Together, we walk to my house for the officers to gather their information and evidence.

Standing inside my kitchen with the police and a now-clothed David, they take down my statement.

"Do you have any enemies?" Officer Pew asks.

"Umm no. None," I say, propping my elbows on my counter, my head in my hands.

"You work as a nurse, you said?"

"Yes. Over at Columbia."

"As a nurse, you lose patients, don't you?" Officer Pew's partner, Officer King, asks in a bored tone.

"I don't see what that has to do with anything." I slap my hands on the marble counter, and a sharp pain goes through my hands.

"Loved ones might blame you for that. Come after you," Officer Pew adds.

"I work on a children's ward. I am close with the children's parents. I just don't see that happening." I pull out a bottle of vodka from my fridge.

"Do you do that often? Perhaps go to bars and pick up men? Men that may get upset with you?" Officer King is really starting to piss me the fuck off.

"I don't go to bars to pick up men. Are we finished here? Obviously, this is going nowhere because I am feeling like I'm being blamed."

"These are standard questions." Officer King writes something in his notepad, as someone calls on the walkie-talkie. He answers it and walks into the living room, with Officer Pew right behind him.

I grab a tall water glass and fill it with vodka. Straight, no chaser needed. Lifting the glass to my lips, my hands tremble and I have to hold the glass steady with both hands in order to take a sip. Officer Pew walks back into the kitchen.

"Well, it seems that another neighbor of yours has reported the same incident. Probably kids playing a joke. Wouldn't worry about it too much if I were you," he says, closing his notepad.

"Wait. That's all?" I ask with what I am sure is a shocked expression on my face.

"Nothing left for us to do. Doubtful we are going to catch the kids who did this." He reaches into his pocket and pulls out a card, and places it on my counter. "Call if anything else happens." They turn and leave me, my mouth hanging open.

David walks over and picks up the card. I snatch it from his outstretched hand and tear it up, throwing the pieces in the trash.

"Should you have done that?" he asks, staring at me as I take another sip from my glass.

"It's obvious they didn't want to be bothered with this. What's the point?"

"I'll help you clean up and then you can stay at my place till we get your window fixed." David walks over to where I keep my broom and dust pan. "Go upstairs and pack a bag. I'll handle this."

I'm filled with relief that I don't have to sweep up a dead rat. "Thank you, David. I don't know how I could possibly repay you."

He smiles at me and walks into the living room to start cleaning. Upstairs, I pack a few things that I might need. I walk to my staircase when a thought hits me. I head back into my bedroom and close the door behind me, dialing from memory the number that I haven't dialed in so long. It is forever etched in my brain because this number was once my lifeline. I listen as it rings, eventually going to voicemail. "Hi, it's me. Please call me back."

Chapter 5
This Feeling ~ Alabama Shakes

Magnum

She places her hands gently on my lap as she kneels before me. Her eyes are warm with affection as she smiles. "Carl, it's okay. Tell me who did this to you."

I won't tell. I hold my lips tight together for fear words my spill out. Sir will be proud of me because I didn't tell.

She stands and holds her hand out for me. I place my small hand in hers, and she holds it as we walk down the hall to the principal's office. She has me sit with the secretary while she goes behind closed doors to talk to him. I don't know how long they are in there. I look at the clock on the wall, but I can't read the time. I only know the time when the big hand is on twelve, and the little hand is on another number. The secretary gives me a lollipop. Grape, mmm, my favorite. *A buzzing sounds and the secretary stands and takes my hand, and I am led into the principal's office.*

"Carl, have a seat," he says. Mrs. Seton smiles at me, and I know it will be okay. I sit down and continue to lick my lollipop. "Carl, Mrs. Seton says that you have bruising on your back. How did you get it, son?"

My lips tighten around my lollipop as I swing my legs back and forth since my feet can't touch the ground.

"He refuses to talk about it," Mrs. Seton explains. "I think he's being beaten." She tries to whisper the words, but I can hear them just the same.

"Well I've called his parents and they should be here shortly." He pushes away from his desk in his swivel chair. I like swivel chairs. Sir has one in his office at home. When Sir is at work, I like to turn around and around till I get dizzy.

****

"CJ." My mother shakes my arm. "CJ, son, snap out of it. The doctor was talking to us," my mother scolds. I blink back to the present, startled, and realize I'm not that five-year-old child holding Sir's secret. I look down at Sir hooked up to the machines helping to keep him alive. I fight the urge to disconnect them.

"I was saying that he's stable. We anticipate being able to take him off the ventilator tomorrow since he is making great progress."

Fuck, I flew fourteen hours from Amsterdam back to New York to hear this shit? He's going to live? I shove my hands in my pocket and lean against the wall, not saying a word.

"That's great news, doctor. Isn't it CJ?" my mother asks as she bends over and kisses my father's cheek.

"Yeah, real fucking great. We done here?" This room suddenly feels far too small for the four of us, and I'm having trouble breathing.

"You okay?" The doc pulls out his pocket light, and I shake my head. "You look as if you might collapse."

"Don't worry about me. Worry about that son of a bitch lying in bed over there. I'm just jet-lagged." I straighten and walk towards the door. "I need some air. I'll be back in a few." I don't bother to wait for either of them to respond as I bolt out the door and down the hall, still fighting to breathe. I haven't set sights on Sir since I was seventeen years old when I left home. Swore I was never going to look at that son of a bitch again, but I kept in touch with my mom. She would find ways to meet me when Sir wasn't around. But seeing him lying in that bed, hooked up to those machines, is bringing everything back to me. Things from my childhood that I'm still not prepared to deal with.

I press the button for the elevator and wait anxiously for it to come. The elevator finally arrives, and I step on, where I'm given a wide berth by those in the car, as usual. As soon as the doors close, I can breathe again. I rub a hand over my shaved scalp.

"Magnum?" I hear a voice I haven't heard in a long time. I turn around and see her. Nurse Brenda Johnson, Cyma's best friend. She is still sexy as hell, even in that nurse's uniform.

"Oh hey, Brenda. Didn't see you," I say, taking a step closer to her. She seems to slink deeper into the corner at my approach. Her hazel eyes have a flicker of something in them.

"What are you doing here?" She averts her eyes.

Shit. I really fucked up when I stopped returning her calls. She looks so delicate and fragile, and I couldn't imagine doing the things to her that I usually do to my bedmates. Brenda seems to be the type that you marry; not the spank'em, fuck'em and leave'em type.

"Sir had a heart attack," I explain. The elevator doors open and we are suddenly alone.

"Sir?"

I'm not used to calling him anything else but Sir, but I'll be damned if he was ever a father. "Yeah, the sperm donor," I say nonchalantly.

"Oh, your father." She smiles.

"No. The sperm donor," I correct her. She lowers her head. *Jesus, I'm a fucking asshole.* "Sorry. Didn't mean to take it out on you."

"It's okay." The elevator door opens again. She walks toward it, placing her hand on the door, so it doesn't close. "I hope he gets better soon." She turns to leave, but I don't want her to go. I don't want to be alone, needing someone to talk to for a bit. I place my hand on her shoulder, and she tenses.

"Can you grab a cup of coffee with me? I know I don't deserve for you to be nice to me, but it would help get my mind off shit." I play with my tongue ring as I wait for her response.

"Well, I still have my shift to finish." She looks down the hall, and I realize we're on the children's ward. I remember coming here several times when Cyma and Tick's daughter Lelia was here.

"Hey, I'll even let you take a swing at me for not returning your phone calls if you like."

She laughs at my comment. "I have to get someone to cover me, and I can't stay long."

"Deal," I reply and place my hand on the small of her back, as we walk off the elevator together. Brenda has curves in all the right places. She isn't fat, but she is a brick house. She reaches around and pushes my hand away.

"Just because I agreed to coffee doesn't mean I agreed to anything else. Let's be clear about that." She glares at me. I stop and laugh as I watch her walk away to talk to another nurse. I forgot Brenda has some fire to her. My dick twitches at this revelation as I imagine fucking her from behind, her hands tied to my bed. She finishes talking to the nurse and walks back over to me.

I bow slightly and chuckle. "After you." She swats at me and walks towards the elevator and presses the button. The bell chimes and a doctor steps through the opening doors. He is reading something but looks up and smiles at Brenda.

The smile he gives her makes me want to put him in the hospital as a patient.

"Break?"

A blush forms on her cheeks. *What the fuck is he to her?*

"Yes, a quick one." She points from him to me. "Doc-"

"Ray," he corrects.

"Ray, this is Magnum." She now points from me to him. "Magnum, this is Doctor Raymond Cross."

Something is going on between these two, and it might be something between the sheets. I mumble a quick hello and reach out, not to shake his outstretched hand but to catch the elevator so we can get the hell out of here.

"Nice to meet you, Doc. But Bren here promised me a quick cup of coffee. You don't want to hold her up too much, do you? She has to get back to her shift, after all." My voice oozes sarcasm like an oil slick.

Brenda shoots me an angry glare before passing an apologetic look to doctor what's-his-face. As soon as the door is closed, she punches me in the arm. I hold back a laugh because honestly, it was cute. We ride the rest of the way in silence.

Minutes later, we are sitting in the hospital's cafeteria, drinking some of the worse coffee I've ever had in my life. Some people stare at us and whisper. I'm used to the stares; having facial piercings, and tats on my shaved head usually attract the weird looks. Brenda never seems to be phased by it. I remember the first time I saw her in Cyma's old building lobby. When our eyes locked, I felt that she saw me, the real me. My past, my present, and my future shown in her eyes. That shit both intrigued me and scared me, all at once.

"I'm sorry for not returning your calls. You're a nice girl and all, but…"

She holds her hand up. "First thing's first, I'm not a girl. I'm a woman. Next, keep your apology for not returning my calls to yourself. You wouldn't have thought to apologize if it weren't for the fact that you ran into me today. You weren't into me. I get it. And it's okay. I didn't lose sleep over it, so get over yourself." She places her hand back down and takes a sip of her coffee.

Nurse Brenda Johnson has more depth all of a sudden. "I stand corrected." I straighten in my seat.

"Besides, you were under the impression that I wanted a relationship with you?" She rolls her eyes at me. "Puh-leeze. I was hoping to get a good fuck out of you. I don't do relationships."

Stunned, I sit back in my seat, my mouth agape. "Funny. Neither do I," I tell her honestly.

"Oh well. Looks like you missed out. I've moved on to the next." She sits back in her seat with a wicked gleam in her eye. What the fuck? Moved on with who? With the doctor? I'm about to ask her when she stands suddenly. "Your time is up. I have to get back to work." She dumps her cup in the garbage and turns back around. "I really do hope your fa-I mean, sperm donor, gets well soon. See you around, Magnum." She spins around and saunters out of the cafeteria with an extra sashay in her step, perhaps telling me to kiss her ass, or lick it. I'm thinking both.

Chapter 6
That Don't Impress Me Much ~ Shania Twain

Brenda

"Bren, I feel so bad that you're picking up all these extra shifts," my co-worker Maritza pouts as I file a patient's folder away.

"Oh, don't worry about it. Really I don't mind it at all," I explain as I rub the back of my neck. The bottom line is, I hate being home by myself. When I'm alone, I'm left to think, and to remember. At least when I'm working, it keeps my mind off my demons. I look up and glance at the wall calendar, eyeing the quickly approaching date. A shiver goes through me, and I rub my hands against my arms, feeling the prickly goosebumps that have popped up. The anniversary is coming, and I can't bear the thought of being home alone on that day.

"Bren. I owe you one. I really do. My husband and I haven't had a romantic getaway in, I don't know when. I still can't believe that I scored those tickets from the radio station."

I close the file cabinet and lean against it, crossing my arms over my chest. "Guess it pays to be a loyal listener."

"Tell me about it. I've been calling that station for *years*, hoping to be the lucky caller, and finally, I win." She smiles brightly, clapping her hands together.

"Well, I hope the two of you have fun. Have a drink or two for me," I tell her as I walk around the nurse's station, preparing for my rounds.

I check in on a few of my patients, checking their vitals and comforting the parents of some. Closing a patient's door behind me, I turn to walk to the next room when I hear my name roll off the lips of the man I'm not sure if I'm anxious or pissed to hear from, yet again.

I turn around with a glare. "This is the children's ward, Magnum."

A gleam is in his eyes as he smirks at me. "Really?" He looks up and down the hall. "Must've lost my way."

"I guess the Disney characters on the wall didn't give it away." I raise my finger and point past him. "Elevators are down the hall and to your left."

"I'm a blockhead for directions, you know. You might have to show me." Humor dances across his face and I'm not sure if I want to kiss or slap that pierced mouth of his. Deep in my own thoughts, my tongue playfully licks across my lips, daydreaming they are his instead. Looking up, I see him staring at my actions, and I stow my tongue back in its place.

"What do you want?" I walk away from him, not waiting to see if he's following.

I hear his long strides behind me till he is next to me. His body heat radiates off of him and clings to me like a caress. I shake my head lightly to ward off the spell he has over me.

"Came to give you a real apology. I was an asshole a few nights ago. Shit, I was just an asshole all the way around with you, and for that, I'm sorry."

Damn it. It was so much easier to be upset with him when he was being a dick, but now he's being nice and leaving me no other choice but to be nice as well. I lift my hand to rub my weary neck.

He reaches out and wraps his fingers gently around my wrist, pulling me closer to him. Kissing my wrist softly, it sends tingles through me. "This is a genuine apology. You deserved better than the shit I was dishing. You saw through it and called me out on it. Gotta respect the truth. That is one of the things that turns me on about you. You have a 'take no prisoners' approach, and that is sexy as fuck."

My breath catches in my throat, and I avert my eyes, pulling my wrist from his grasp. "So sexy that you stopped calling? Magnum, it doesn't matter. Really, it doesn't. When I said I don't do relationships, I wasn't trying to save face in front of you. I really don't do relationships. I was digging you and thought you felt the same. Thought we could have some fun together. It didn't work out, so that's the end of it. Nothing to cry about. You're off the hook; no apology is needed. Did it hurt my ego? Yes. But I'm over it."

He stares at me for a long moment as my heart pounds feverishly in my chest. "Looks like I'm not the only one who's running," he says so low he is barely audible.

My mouth goes dry, and my heart feels like it is now in my throat. Am I really that transparent? "What are you running from?" Most likely the cops.

"Who, me? I run from nothing. I always run into the fight." He crosses his arms as his bicep muscles flex, and I can't help but stare at the artwork on his arms.

"What's the story behind the art?" I want to reach out and trace my fingers over the lines but stop myself.

"I usually share that story after I've fucked a girl. But you, I guess I can share with after a drink." He gives me a cocky grin. One of my fellow nurses walks by, staring at us, and gives me a thumbs up behind him as she walks away.

"Well since we're not fucking, and I refuse to have a drink with you, I guess I'll just make up a story on my own." I tap my finger on my chin. "Oh, I know. You're a wanna be badass. Bet you got the tats and the piercings just to impress the ladies." My tone drips with sarcasm.

He throws his head back in laughter. "Damn, I love that smart mouth of yours."

I grumble under my breath and look over to see Maritza waving for me to come over to the nurse's station. I walk around the jerk and towards Maritza. There is a delivery person holding a long white box with a bow on it, waiting.

"Are you Brenda Johnson?" the delivery person asks.

I eye him suspiciously before nodding. He hands me a slip to sign. I look from it to the delivery person, wondering who would be sending me flowers. I sign, and he hands me the box.

"Looks like flowers, Bren." Maritza claps her hands together, eagerly waiting for me to open the box. "You didn't tell me you were dating!"

"Yeah, you didn't tell me you were dating," Magnum says from behind. "Don't tell me I have competition." He stands in front of me with a wicked grin.

"Oh please, Mag." I inhale deeply as I contemplate who the sender could be. Maybe Ray, or perhaps Magnum sent it and is making like he didn't, to throw me off. Placing the box on the desk, I untie the bow. As I lift the lid, I hold back a scream as I jump away. Twenty dead flowers with the message "Happy Anniversary."

Magnum moves me behind him and holds up the box, before throwing it back onto the desk and running down the hall, most likely trying to catch the delivery person. I feel numb as I stand immobile, trying not to cry out in panic. I turn around to see if *he* is there. But he can't be.

"Oh, my God, Bren. Who would do such a thing?" Maritza wraps her arms around my shoulders. I lean into her, grateful for the support because I can no longer feel my legs.

My lips begin to tremble as I try to find words to speak. Finding the strength to move, I continue to back away from the desk until I hit a wall behind me and slowly slide to the floor. Footsteps pound down the hall and I feel muscular arms lift me up. I'm too much in a daze to pay it any attention.

"Bring her in here." I hear a worried voice.

I'm placed on the couch in the nurse's room, and hear activity around me, but am unable to focus.

"Brenda. Are you okay?" Light is shined in my eyes, and I blink rapidly.

"Y-yes. I just need a minute."

My wrist is held in Ray's hand as he takes my pulse. "Your pulse is rapid. Just lay here until you are feeling better, then I think you should go home."

A tremble goes through me at the thought of going home alone. I blink back tears. Throughout the chaos, I haven't realized my head is resting on Magnum's lap. His strong hands cover me protectively, as his fingers run gently through my hair. "It's alright. Anyone who wants to get to you has to get through me first."

I look up to see the serious expression on his face. He has made a declaration for all to hear that he would give his life to protect me. For once, with his words, I don't feel alone in this world. But I'm still afraid to give him my trust; I need to be strong for myself. God knows I've learned that the hard way.

Ray looks from me back to Magnum, his eyes full of hurt, and I'm too stunned to say anything, to right the situation that he thinks is going on.

"I need a moment alone with her." Magnum's voice is full of command like a five-star general.

The nurses nod their heads and exit the room. Ray stands there and waits for me to give him the signal that I am okay to be alone with Magnum. *Am I okay?* I eventually give him the nod, and he leaves without a word. We sit in silence for a long time; me, listening to his breaths as a way to calm my own and him, probably lost in thought. Eventually, I feel strong enough to swing my legs to the floor and sit up. He releases me with slight hesitation.

"Wanna tell me what the dead flowers are about?" His voice a low thunder.

I shake my head, praying for the memories to fall out of my brain and splatter on the floor beside my feet. For so long, I've tried to live this double life. Thinking I could run, no, hide from my past and here it is, coming back to me.

He stands up quickly and hovers over me, making me feel like a disobedient child. From this angle, the hoop ring in his nose gives him an imposing look. I lower my head and look at the floor.

"Ex-boy toy upset with you or something, since you don't do the boyfriend thing?" His nostrils flare.

"No." I close my eyes in hopes if I wish him away, he'd disappear. I open my eyes, but he is still standing in front of me, his eyes as piercing as ever.

"Usually women get flowers of the live variety. For a tough as nails chick, your reaction was of terror. Trust me, I know what it looks like. Is someone after you?"

"No." I place my hands on my temples, looking down again. "I don't know." I can't risk telling him the truth. I couldn't bear the look of shock that would inevitably cover his face and the judgmental look that would follow. I tighten my lips and place my trembling hands on my knees.

"Should we get the cops involved?" he asks hesitantly.

I think back to my case officers from last week that handled my broken window. They all but accused me of deserving whatever I got without knowing who I was. Nope, I am not subjecting myself to that again. "No. No cops. I just need to get back to work. I'm fine."

"You heard the doctor. He said for you to go home." He glares at me.

"Don't want to go home."

He steps back and looks at me appraisingly. "You're afraid to go home, aren't you?"

I swallow hard and look toward the door, wondering how I can get away.

He exhales and cracks his knuckles. "You're so forthcoming with information. I'll take you home and crash on your couch."

My head jerks up to look at him. "Wh-what?"

He steps closer to me, his hand extended, waiting for me to take it. "You heard me. Come on, let's go."

I contemplate arguing with him, but I can see he won't budge on this. Reluctantly I place my hand in his and stand. "I need to grab my stuff."

"From where?"

I nod my head in the direction of my locker. "Over there."

"Alright. I'll be here."

I go into the adjacent room and quickly grab my stuff before this hulking man comes barreling in the room to make sure I'm okay. When I get back to the room, he's standing by the door.

"Okay, I'm ready." He turns to look at me and nods. Placing a protective hand on the small of my back, he guides me out of the hospital and safely deposits me into his car. An hour later, we arrive at my house and I take out my keys, but his large fingers gently remove them from my fingertips.

"Stand behind me. I'll go in first," he whispers, and without argument, I do as he says. He removes his gun I wasn't aware he had and unlocks my door. I wait outside as he does a sweep of my house. He comes back to the door with his gun holstered again. "Come on in. It's clear."

I step inside, thankful he searched for the boogeyman that has most likely found me. Walking into my living room, I toss my purse on the couch and go straight to the kitchen. Without asking, I pour us both a shot of Belvedere straight. Not hearing, but knowing he is behind me, I turn to hand him his glass, which he willingly accepts. I lean against the counter as I savor the burning liquid going down my throat.

"You should get some rest." He finishes his drink and sets the now empty glass on the counter.

The mention of rest instantly makes my body slouch. I didn't realize how tired I was. "I'll get you set up in the guest room."

A wicked gleam comes over his eyes. "What, not inviting me to share your bed? I'd be more effective protecting you if I was in the same room with you."

I grab his glass and place it in the sink with my empty one. "Not a chance, big boy," I say, as I walk past him.

"Can't blame a man for trying," he laughs.

I walk up the steps with him behind me. "You can choose whichever room you want. The sheets are fresh."

"If it's okay with you, I'll sleep on the couch. Just in case."

I turn to look at him, and for the first time, I notice the bags under his eyes. "But you'll be more comfortable in a bed, won't you?"

"I'm good. Just give me a sheet and pillow. I'll make do."

I purse my lips together to stop the remark that's itching to come out. Instead, I turn back around and grab some sheets from the linen closet. I make up the couch for him and step back to admire my handiwork. Satisfied, I head upstairs to shower and then sleep.

****

A loud thud and a crash wakes me from my sleep. At first, I'm not sure if I dreamt the sound as I sit up in my bed, listening.

"What the fuck, man? Who are you? Where is Brenda?" I hear David's voice downstairs. I jump off my bed, not bothering to grab a robe, and run down the stairs. I stop mid-flight at the sight of David faceplanted against the wall, with Magnum twisting one arm behind his back to the point his shoulder bone looks like it will snap.

"Magnum. Stop. It's my next-door neighbor, David!" I yell and run down the final steps.

Magnum looks at me and then back at David, still not letting go of his arm. "You know this nerd?" I choke back a laugh because David does look like the classic nerd you see on television sitcoms. The glasses that never seem to fit right, the pants that are outdated. I've always fancied him to be a cute nerd, actually.

"He's not a nerd. Just let him go."

"Yeah, let me go." Magnum releases David's arm eventually and walks protectively over to me.

"Are you okay?" I ask David. I try to walk over to him, but Magnum places his hand around my waist, holding me in place. For some reason, it comforts me.

David's eyes concentrate on where Magnum's hand is placed. He looks up to meet my eyes but quickly looks away. "Yes, I think," he says as he moves his arm around, wincing at the motions.

"What are you doing here?" I ask.

"I got worried. I knew your shift had ended. Didn't see your car outside. Tried calling your cell but it kept going to voicemail, so I decided to use the spare key you gave me last week to check on you." He looks over to Magnum. "And that's when the thug attacked me." Magnum takes a step towards David, but I hold him back.

"Oh, I'm sorry, David. When I got home, I turned off my cell so I could get some rest." I totally forgot that, after the rat incident, he and I agreed I would check in when I leave and when I come home.

"S'okay, I guess. As long as you are alright."

"She's fine. You can go," Magnum says, and I'm not sure if I should be annoyed or flattered. I decide to be annoyed.

"Magnum...David is a friend of mine. He was just being a good neighbor and making sure I was alright. After the scare last week, he's been a godsend."

His eyes narrow at me. "Scare? What scare?"

I pointedly ignore Magnum and walk over to David. "Come with me so I can look at your arm."

He follows me into the living room and takes a seat on the couch I made up for Magnum to sleep on. The couch that he hasn't been in at all since it's completely untouched. I look over at Magnum, who looks away. I'll have to remember to ask him about that.

"Move your arm this way." I guide it gently. "Hmm, okay, now this way." I guide it in the opposite direction, looking at his facial responses. "I think it is just a sprain. Nothing broken." I place my hands on his and have him flex his fingers. "Ice it for an hour, then off for an hour, and ice again." I rush upstairs to the medicine cabinet and back down before Magnum shoots him or something. I hand some pain killers to David. "Just take two for now, with some food. If needed, you can take again in six hours."

"Thanks," he mumbles and stands up to leave.

"Key," Magnum says, his hand outstretched.

"Huh?" David turns to look at him.

"Key. I'm taking care of Brenda for now on." He doesn't budge from his position.

David looks at me and then back to Magnum. "Only if Brenda is okay with it," he challenges Magnum. *Good for him.*

"Magnum. It's okay for David to have the key. He lives next door and can get to me quicker than you can."

"Till we figure this shit out, no one has the keys. Got me?"

I think about his rationalization, but can't find an argument for it. I nod, sending an apologetic look David's way. He gives me a weak smile and hands the key over to Magnum. Once David leaves, I turn to the big, bossy brute standing in my living room.

"You didn't have to treat him like he was a criminal."

"You fucking him or something? Wouldn't have taken him for your type. You seem like you like it rough. That nerd doesn't look like he can even get it up."

I feel my cheeks warm, and I want to slap him. My Hippocratic Oath comes to mind as I debate throwing something at his head. "You have some nerve. It's none of your business who I fuck."

"My guess is, you're *not* fucking him. If you were, you wouldn't have let me take control the way I did. But, the way he looked at you...either you almost fucked or you talked about fucking."

The slender thread that was holding my temper snaps and I raise my hand to slap him. He catches my wrist and pulls me into him, kissing me fiercely. My mind tells me to push away from him but my damn body reacts to him and pulls him closer. Fuck. My body, the horny bitch; she and I will have a long talk tonight. I playfully tug on his lip piercing, and he groans. Moving his lips away from my own, he bites me on my chin and moves his mouth over to my ear. "Oh, Queen B likes to play, does she? I like it rough too, baby."

My knees feel weak, but I find the strength to back away from him, only to see him grinning from ear to ear. Without another word, I walk around him and back upstairs to my room. I lock my bedroom door to the sound of him laughing.

Chapter 7
Stand By Me ~ The Staple Singers

Magnum

I oversee the workmen installing the security system in Brenda's house as she's asleep upstairs. I'm pretty sure she's going to raise the living dead when she sees what I've done, but keeping her safe is my only priority. Unfortunately, I've got to get back to the hospital to sit with my mother as she waits for Sir to wake. They took him off the machines, but he has been in and out of it, for the most part. I told her the moment he is fully awake, I'm gone. I don't want to look at his evil eyes again; the same eyes that showed hatred for me for as long as I can remember. Hell, I only did this much because of my mother. For him, I could piss on his grave and not give a shit.

"That good, Mag?" my friend Styx asks.

I walk over to inspect his handiwork. "Yeah, looks good. The feed goes to the TV and cell, right?"

"Yep. Also, nothing getting in here unless it's an armored truck."

"Good." We pound it out. "I owe you one for coming out on such short notice."

"She must be someone important for you to call me at three in the morning," he says while packing up his tools.

"She is." I say the words so quickly my brain and mouth haven't caught up to each other. When I see the strange look he gives me, I clear my throat. "She's Tick's old lady's best friend."

Styx doesn't say a word; just goes back to packing. As he finishes, I catch him staring at something behind me. I turn around to see a confused Brenda walking down the steps in nothing but her sleep tank and shorts. Styx looks her over, and I have to stop myself from laying him the fuck out. Why doesn't she put on some clothes? She ran downstairs like that last night in front of the nerd...David, was his name?

"Hey, I'm Styx," he says, walking over to the steps with his hand outstretched. She looks at me and then takes his hand.

"Brenda?" She says her name like a question.

"Sorry that you have to go so fast, Styx, but thanks for the favor." I'm not liking the way he is looking at her one bit, and I can't be held responsible for my actions.

"Oh but..." I don't give him a chance to finish as I manhandle him towards the door and close it in his face.

Turning to look at her, my eyes drift to her erect nipples through her tank. *Focus, Magnum, focus.* "Don't you ever wear clothes?" My voice comes out angrier than I mean for it to be.

She blinks back the shock of my tone. "I'm in my own house. Why was this Styx person here with what looked like a tool bag?"

Relieved she has given me something to focus on instead of her nipples, I answer her. "He installed a security system." I hold my hand out to her, which she reluctantly takes. Walking her over to the keypad, I show her how it works.

"Mag, I don't need one. This is a quiet block. Why would you do this? You didn't even ask me."

"Had to. You're not safe. This is a state of the art system. Besides, I have to run to the hospital to visit Sir for a few hours. Needed to make sure you're good till I get back."

"You've already done too much, Mag." She pouts at me.

"Nah. Not enough. Promise me you'll take this shit seriously. I know you haven't felt comfortable enough to tell me what the problem is...but just know that I'm here when you're ready to talk."

She looks down at her hands before lifting her head and smiling at me. Her eyebrows knit together and I turn to see what she is staring at. "You haven't slept."

Of course, she's looking at the couch that I never bothered to use. How do I explain that I can't sleep because I have a fear of my dreams, memories that haunt me? Memories, courtesy of Sir.

"Wanted to stay alert just in case something or someone tried to get in." I partially tell the truth, and she seems appeased by my answer.

"I feel bad that you lost sleep because of me. Why don't you lay down for a little bit before you head out?"

"Can't. Promised my mother I would meet her and I'm already running late. I won't be long. Here is my cell if you need me. And don't let anyone in. Not even the nerd." I hand her a card with my cell number on it.

"His name is David." She rolls her eyes at me.

"Yeah, whatever. David to you, nerd to the rest of the world. Don't let him in."

"He's harmless, and was there for me when I needed him last week."

"'Bout that. What happened last week?"

She turns away and walks toward the front window. "Nothing."

"Well, it was something where you needed his help, so spill." I shove my hands in my pockets as I wait for her to talk, knowing I'm running late but unable to make myself leave before hearing the answer.

"Someone threw a rock, with a dead rat attached, through my front window. But the cops told me that a few of my neighbors complained about the same thing, so it was probably just kids playing a prank. I had to stay at David's house a few nights while my window was fixed."

My pulse quickens at the possible threat to her. I grab my gun from my holster and hold it up. "Know how to use this?"

"N-no. I don't want it." She places her hands behind her back.

I walk over and reach around her to gently tug at her wrist. I feel her breasts rub against my chest and for a moment, I forget what I was doing. Eventually, she relaxes and I place the gun in her hand. "For now, if danger is coming your way, you can just point it at a fucker, and that should buy you some time to get away. I'll teach you how to use it this week." She hesitates before she wraps her fingers around the handle. "You see this?" She nods. "That's the safety." I flip the safety down. "That removes it, and you are ready to rock and roll." I stand behind her and help her to balance the gun in her hand. "I doubt you'll have to shoot, but if you do, this is what you do." I position her body against mine and show her how to aim. "This is just a quickie. I'll show you more during the week." Her body flush against mine feels good, really good, and it takes everything in me not to carry her upstairs and fuck her senseless. I have the feeling she needs it as much as I do.

She turns around, and we are face to face staring at each other. "Thank you, Mag."

I stare at her plump lips that, just hours ago, I had against mine. Her taste is even better than I remember from the frantic kiss we shared last year. Her eyes look anxiously at me, and something passes between us. I pull her into me quickly and take a nip at her bottom lip. She smiles and places her free hand on my chest, pushing me away gently.

"You can shower upstairs before you go. Fresh towels are laid out for you." She smiles.

I take the gun from her and double check that the safety is on before handing it back to her. "Keep this near you at all times." She nods as she takes the gun back and places it on the end table.

I go upstairs to quickly shower, and when I come downstairs, I see that she has company. Not the nerd but another asshole. The doctor.

She turns as I reach the last step.

"Good shower?" she asks.

I don't respond as I stare at the good ol' doc sitting next to her on the couch. *Seriously, did they fuck?*

He clears his throat. "I came by to check on our Brenda. She gave us quite the scare yesterday." He places his arm around her. I know this move; he's marking his territory, letting me know that she's his, and I need to back off.

If it's a pissing match he wants, trust me, I can piss longer than the best of them.

I remain silent as I stare at his arm around her and contemplate if I should break it or just snatch it off.

"Mag." I blink and look at Brenda. "Didn't you say you had to go to be with your mom?" She turns to the doctor. "His father had a heart attack and is a patient at our hospital."

The doctor looks at me with mock sympathy and smiles. "Who is his doctor? I can check on him, if you like, or consult with his attending physician."

Listen to this brown-nosing motherfucker.

Before I can say anything, Brenda interrupts, her voice panicked by what my reply would be. "Thank you so much, Ray. I'm sure Mag appreciates all that. Let's let him get back to his family, and I'll give you those details later." She rises and grabs my arm and, with a little more force than necessary, makes me turn around as she walks me towards the door.

I have a good mind to take a seat and make him sweat, but I did promise my mother that I was on my way.

I look at her when we stop in front of the door. "Call me if you need me," I say loudly, making sure Doctor Bullshit hears me. "You felt so fucking good in my arms last night. I hope to have a repeat of that tonight." I watch the color drain from the doctor's face. Yeah, I think I've won this pissing match.

She plasters on a fake smile and hisses, "What the hell are you doing?" She glares at me, and I want to take her and fuck some sense into her head while screaming, "You see Doctor Shithead, this is the way I mark *my* territory."

"Nothing, I just wanted to thank you for that incredible kiss last night. You did feel good against me." *Too damn good*, I think to myself.

"Thank you for everything, and I hope he gets better soon. I'll see you later. Don't worry about me; Ray is here," she replies, just as loudly, and I grumble.

For some reason, I feel gutted when she says that. Can Ray make the bad men disappear for her? Will Ray take care of her the way I could? Could Ray make her scream out his name the way I know I would?

Fuck Ray. I open the door so hard that it slams against the wall. Without turning around, I walk to my car and drive to the hospital with a 'Fuck Ray' mantra going in my head.

***

Hours later, I'm sitting with my mother in Sir's room, listening to the machines beep. She was upset with me for leaving abruptly last night. I told her I was getting some coffee, which was my intention until Brenda received the dead roses and changed my plans. Besides, there is no love lost between Sir

63

and I. I'm here for my mother and not that son of a bitch lying in that bed. My mother has always been a weak woman. She never stood up to Sir and would always take his abuse. He never hit her the way he would me, like I was his own personal punching bag. His abuse towards her was the mental and verbal kind. He hurled insults at her like it was his job.

I remember when I was a kid, I once saw a picture of my mom when she was young and single. She was a knockout, and could've had any man she wanted. But instead, she settled for an Army man who never could make it up the ranks. He made it to Corporal and never could move higher. As his friends went on to become Majors and Colonels, he remained a lowly Corporal, forever overlooked by his commanding officers. Mom said he wasn't always like this. He was a good man at one time. She said he changed gradually over the years; probably from being passed over on promotions that were promised and never happened. When he decided to retire from active duty, he remained in the reserves to always be close to the military; his main claim to fame. Once he became a civilian, life wasn't much better, as he could never find a really decent job. Again, he was never considered for promotions, and when layoffs came, he was always the first to be let go. By the time I was born, my father was a hard and bitter man. He was angry at the world for overlooking him and his potential. Potential that he sought to put in me, that he beat into me. What the world failed to see in him, he was going to make sure they didn't do the same to his son.

He pushed and pushed for me to excel, especially in sports. His dream was for me to go pro in basketball. When my friends were allowed to play outside, I was made to train with my father on the court. When he took me as far as he could, he hired a trainer. No one was going to overlook his kid. If I missed a shot, he would beat me. If I was late to practice, he used his fists to remind me how important it was to be punctual. My father's punishments came down hard and brutal. Because he became a father-like figure to so many fatherless boys in my neighborhood, he was beyond reproach. No one could ever imagine he would beat his kid. No one. No matter how many bruises I went to school with, or unexplained broken bones, it was all brushed aside because an outstanding citizen like my father could never do such a thing.

Mom even fed into the bullshit as I cried at night in the darkness of my room. She'd sneak into my room when Sir was sleeping, to soothe away my silent tears. Always telling me how lucky I was to have a father who loved me so much. That I must be understanding and patient with him. Now here I am staring at Sir lying in bed, looking helpless, and the only thing I wish for is his death.

"When your father wakes, we can be a family again. I've prayed for this for so many years, CJ," my mother says as she pats my knee.

I tense at her words and fight the urge to shove her hand away. "Only here for you. Not this piece of shit," I say through gritted teeth.

Her hand flies to her lips as she lets out a loud gasp. "CJ. He is your *father*."

I stand abruptly, and the chair makes a screeching sound across the floor. "Father? No, he is no father to me. That is Sir." I point a finger to the now old man lying in bed. "Stop feeding me the bullshit, Mom. He hates me just like I hate him.

If you didn't stop me..." I don't finish the sentence because I feel a slap across my face. It doesn't hurt, though. It probably hurt her more than it did me.

"Don't you say it." She shakes her fist at me, tears streaming down her face.

"Mom...I..."

"You don't have to be here, CJ. Just leave. I thought, because of this, the two of you could make amends. But I see you can't move forward."

"How do you choose him over me? Every time? I needed you all those years when he was beating the fucking shit out of *me*. You stood by and let him do it. You *let* me be his punching bag."

"He is my *husband*." Her words come out with a tremble.

I stab my finger into my chest, wishing it was a knife. That shit would be easier than this. "I'm your *son*." My voice rises a pitch higher then I intended, and an astonished look crosses my mother's face.

"Excuse me? Is everything alright in here?" A nurse peeks her head in the doorway.

My mother wipes the tears away from her cheeks. "Yes. My son was just leaving. He, unfortunately, can't stay to see his father and was telling me goodbye." My mother's words explain the noise to the nurse, all the while dismissing me.

The nurse looks at my mother and me before she steps fully into the room. She checks my father's vitals and quickly exits again. My mother walks over to my father's bedside and holds his hand in hers. There are so many questions I have for my mother, but I'm afraid to ask them. Me, a man who has blood on my hands, afraid to ask his own mother how she could let daddy hit me. Maybe Sir was right all along; perhaps I *am* a pussy. Without another word, I leave, my warring emotions stirring inside me. I look at my cell for the time and see that I have several missed phone calls from Tony. I can't deal with him tonight, so I decide to ignore them. I need to get my shit under control before I head back to Brenda's house. I walk towards the elevators when my cell phone rings.

I close my eyes momentarily and mutter under my breath before answering, not bothering to look at the caller ID. "Yeah?"

"Cyma went into labor. We're all meeting up at the hospital," Brenda says over the phone.

Chapter 8

Anything (Remix) ~ SWV Feat. Wu-Tang Clan

Brenda

Cyma gave birth to a healthy baby girl that they named Hope. Lelia is so excited that she is now a big sister, and I've never seen Tick look so anxious and scared until he held his daughter in his arms. Cyma and Hope are due home today, so Anaya and I are getting the house ready for their homecoming. It is just a small gathering of family and friends. Tick's parents came down from Upstate and will be staying for a month. They wanted to help Cyma and Tick as much as they can.

"Okay, I think I hear them pulling up in the driveway," Anaya says, as she puts away the step ladder we were using to hang the welcome home sign.

"Great. I'll get the door for them." I rush across the living room to open it.

The family is getting out of the car and are all smiles. Tick is carrying Lelia on his shoulders as Cyma holds the baby, and the proud grandparents walk close behind. Cyma looks radiant holding baby Hope. She sees me and beams. I take the baby from her arms; I already have a list of ways I am going to spoil her.

Everyone whispers, careful not to wake the baby. I go upstairs to place Hope down in her crib and set the baby monitor to on. Back downstairs, everyone is hugging the new parents and Lelia.

"Thank you so much, everyone," Cyma beams.

"Babe. You should sit and get some rest." Tick places his arms protectively around his wife.

"I keep telling you I'm fine." She smiles lovingly at him.

"Can I go upstairs and play with the baby?" Lelia asks, while tugging on my dress hem.

I bend down to hug her. "No, sweetheart. The baby is sleeping. When she wakes up, you can play with her." She pouts, but Xavier hits her and runs. Lelia gives chase to Xavier around the house.

"Xavier. Stop running," Anaya calls out with an exasperated sigh.

"I'll get him," Tony says, standing to get his two-year-old son.

Manny, who flew in when he heard that Cyma was in labor, stands up and catches Lelia as she tries to run past him. "Hey, baby girl. Cheating on me already?" he jokes as he holds her in his arms, and she gives him a hug. Tick growls in the background, and Manny laughs even louder. He mock whispers, "Don't tell dad that I'm your favorite guy okay."

Lelia smiles brightly at him. "Okay. Pinky swear." They seal it with their two pinkies crossed together.

Magnum stands off by himself in a corner, looking detached from the festivities. Occasionally he takes a sip of his drink, but mostly stares off into the distance. Ever since he went to visit his father in the hospital, he has been off, almost like he is in a constant deep thought. Every now and then, he breaks out of his funk, but neither his laugh nor his smile really seem genuine. Like a knee jerk reaction. I should know; I've been known to do this myself every now and then. Also, from what I can gather, he still hasn't slept, but I haven't asked him about it for fear he would tell me it's none of my business. Secrets are one thing I can understand since I have some of my own.

Cyma walks over to me and whispers quietly, "What's with you and Magnum?"

"Huh?" I shift from one foot to the other.

"Oh, don't play dumb with me. You've been looking over at him for most of the afternoon."

"Have I?" I ask, lifting my glass to my lips, in an attempt to hide my embarrassment at being caught.

"Yes, you have." She nudges my side, and I giggle.

"Fine, I was just wondering why he's standing off by himself."

"Oh, that's all?" She looks over at him and then back to me, leaning in closer. "He has a habit of doing that when the kids are around. I don't think he likes kids or something like that."

Stunned, I look over at him again and stare. He picks this moment to look at me and our eyes lock. He is a hard ass, and I know he has most likely killed for the people in this room, but he has a compassionate side to him. I've seen it firsthand. I just can't believe he doesn't like children. Without breaking our gaze, I say to Cyma, "I don't believe that."

"Well, I don't know. He acts very weird whenever the kids are around. Tick also mentioned that he refuses to be left alone with the kids. I haven't even seen him so much as talk to Lelia or Xavier. Not even pick them up. Those two kids are adorable. Who *doesn't* love them?"

A questioning look appears in his eyes, and I smile at him. He returns the smile before turning to look at whatever Manny is doing to entertain the kids. "Does he have any siblings? Nieces or nephews?"

She places her finger on her chin. "Hmm, not that I know of. But he also doesn't talk about his past. Tick has said that on a few occasions. The most I know is that he's loyal to Tony and our family, but no one really knows about his history."

It dawns on me that even though he has been staying at my place, we never really talked about anything serious or deep. We have superficial conversations, and we flirt, but that's it. I didn't pay much attention to it because I'm usually the person who avoids questions about my past. Magnum and I seem to have something in common.

"You look sexy as fuck. Did you wear that for me?" His voice comes from behind me, for my ears only.

The hairs on the back of my neck stand on end as tingles go through me. I smooth my hands over my dress that I know flatters all of my curves. "You wish," I lie to him. I did have him in mind when I chose this.

"Right. Lie to yourself if you want. But don't lie to me." He smirks at me, now standing by my side.

"So, you're in a better mood?" I taunt.

71

He inhales and relaxes. "Yeah. Guess I am. Sorry for being a miserable fuck the past few days. Had a lot on my mind."

"Anything I can help you with?" I look at him expectantly, waiting to see if he will take me up on my offer to help. Because I'd be there for him in a heartbeat.

He cups my chin in his hand. "Nothing that getting you out of that dress won't cure."

I slap his hand away. "I swear, I just never know when to take you seriously."

He bends to whisper in my ear, his breath tickling my neck. "Oh, but I am serious. As serious as a heart attack."

My head turns instinctively towards his, and our lips brush together. I step back, touching where his lips just brushed my own. "I should be going. I need to get home and get ready for work." I back away even further, anxious to give us some distance.

"I'll follow behind you," he says, but I shake my head at him. I have the feeling if he follows me to the house tonight, I won't be going to work but instead would be underneath him, screaming out his name. And I'm not sure I'm ready for that.

I say my goodbyes quickly, grabbing my purse and hauling ass to my car, needing to break the spell he has over me. Turning on my BMW, the car purrs to life, and I back out of the driveway. I check my rearview mirror every now and then to see if he's following me. Not seeing him, disappointment envelopes me and I could kick myself. *Oh, Brenda sometimes you daydream too much. He was just teasing you, and you fell for it, as usual.* I enter the expressway, eager to get from behind this slow car in front of me. Another glance in my rearview mirror shows Magnum's car behind me, and my heart does a pitter-patter. Perhaps I didn't imagine it after all. Gunning it, I move over to the middle lane, and he keeps pace. *Oh okay, he wants to chase me, does he?* I smile, because I'm good at speeding down highways. I have the tickets to prove it. Cutting it close, I move quickly to the left lane, and he is now beside me. I press my foot on the gas pedal, and that's when I hear a loud knocking sound. There are too many cars behind me to stop, so I slow down to move back to the right lane, with Magnum behind me every step of the way. The sound is getting louder, and my wheel begins to shake. Before I get a chance to move over to the shoulder, I feel the impact of my car hitting the car to the side of me as it swerves. I fight for control but nothing I do works. The car hits the railing, bouncing me back into the right lane, where I barely miss hitting Magnum. My airbag inflates, knocking my head back into my seat like a ping pong ball. After a few more spins, the car comes to a stop.

My head is pounding...or is that someone pounding on the window of my car? I'm not sure as I'm in and out of consciousness. I feel someone's arms pull me out of the wreckage and lay me down on the highway.

"Bren. Bren. Talk to me." Magnum presses an ear to my chest to listen for a heartbeat. My eyes slowly flutter open, and the sunlight sends sharp pains through my head, and I quickly close my eyes again. *Ugh, wake me when this is over.*

I lift my hand and touch the top of his head. I feel him stiffen, but then he lifts his head and kisses me. It isn't full of lust, as our other kisses have been. It's something deeper. Something I feel in my core.

"So, this is what a girl has to do to get attention?" I ask, while mentally going through a checklist of any pains I am feeling so I can assess how injured I am.

"Damn babe, if attention is all you wanted, you should have just asked instead of going full speed into a guard rail."

"I called 9-1-1. An ambulance should be here shortly." I hear someone standing in the small group of people that has gathered around my accident on the highway.

"Babe. What happened? It looked like you lost control of the car or something." He holds my hand and searches my eyes, waiting for an answer.

"'Or something' is right. I remember hearing a loud knocking sound. That's why I tried to get over to the shoulder. Then I felt a hard impact before I hit the guardrail."

His eyebrows furrow as he listens to me recount what I can remember. A police officer comes over to where I am laying on the ground and talks to Magnum, myself, and any other witnesses. Everyone's story is pretty much the same, with the exception of me being the only one who heard a loud knocking. The police officer takes a look at my car and comes back to us.

"Looks like one of your back wheels came off. Not sure if that's a result of the crash or what actually caused it. When we get the car towed, and the mechanic looks at it, they can tell us which happened first. You are a very lucky lady, ma'am."

"Yes, I know," I reply as the paramedic loads me on to a stretcher. Magnum must have called Tony while we waited because I see him and Manny standing with Magnum, who is apparently explaining what happened. I watch as Manny settles into the driver's side of Magnum's car while Magnum climbs into the back of the ambulance beside me.

A few hours later, I wake up in a hospital room, with Magnum sitting in a chair next to my bed. I'm groggy from the medication that they gave me, and my mouth feels like cotton.

"You waited," I whisper.

A wide smile spreads across his face, and he stands up, taking my hand into his. "Of course I did. The rest of the gang is in the waiting room."

I close my eyes, unsure of all the attention I am getting. I've learned to live my life under the radar, not drawing attention to myself, and now I seem to be the center of it once again.

"You okay? Not feeling well? Want me to call the doc or something?" He shoots off his questions in rapid fire procession.

"No. I'm fine. It's just that I don't want people to worry."

"Let us worry about that. You concentrate on healing."

I lift my hand in search of his. He takes mine into his own and kisses it. "Doc said you have a minor concussion. We can bust you out of this joint tomorrow."

"I feel fine. I can leave now." I shift in the bed to sit up a little.

He presses his hands gently on my shoulders, forcing me to lie back down. "Doc said tomorrow, so tomorrow it is. I'll sleep in here to make sure you don't go all rogue and shit."

Smart man, because as soon as I had a moment, I definitely would've checked myself out of here. The drugs take effect, and I drift off to sleep. But for the first time in a long time, it's a sleep without nightmares.

Chapter 9
<u>Human ~ Rag'n Bone Man</u>

Magnum

Sir and mommy arrive at the principal's office. He looks like an angry giant from where I'm seated. Quickly, I look away from Sir and concentrate on swinging my legs, gaining momentum as I go, accidentally kicking Principal Martinez's desk. I murmur an apology and go back to swinging my legs, this time not as high.

"What's the meaning of pulling me out of work early?" Sir looks me up and down before turning his gaze back to Principal Martinez. "He looks fine."

"Mr. Miller, it has been reported by Carl's teacher that he has bruises on his back. We tried to question him about ..."

"Wait a God damn minute here. You questioned my son without me being present? You've got some fucking nerve," my father's voice booms in the small office. Principal Martinez eyes widen, and his mouth drops open.

Mrs. Seton pulls me into her, I think more as a comfort to her than for me. My mother's stare is blank; she didn't flinch, not once.

"Mr. Miller, our policy is to call social services in a matter like this. But because you are such an outstanding member of this community, we decided to speak to you first." Principal Martinez blinks rapidly as he tries to explain to Sir the reason why he was summoned to the principal's office.

"Police?" He looks over at me, I make sure to not show any fear. If I show fear, it's a sign of weakness, and in our house, there are no weak people. He turns back to Principal Martinez, who my father would consider weak by every definition. He is a small man with a nasally voice, whose glasses are often crooked. "You would call the police for what? A few bruises on his back? I had worse when I was a kid. Is he clothed and fed and brought to school every day? Those are the things you need to worry about."

"But Mr. Miller, how did Carl get those bruises?"

For a moment, my father pauses as he takes the last available seat, leaving my mother to remain standing. "Well, that's easy to explain. Carl and that damn neighbor's kid were rough-housing the other day. When I saw the bruises, I went next door and I gave that boy's parents the business. Trust me, that won't be happening again."

My father doesn't bother to try to hide that he's lying. He drivels off the details like he was reading a shopping list. He sets his jaw, as he sits back in his chair and narrows his eyes at Principal Martinez. Almost as if taunting the small man to say that he's lied. A crooked smile appears on Sir's face, and he winks at Principal Martinez. A small bead of sweat forms on my principal's brow. He takes out his handkerchief and wipes his forehead, then cleans his glasses.

"I see," he says after he clears his throat.

My father stands and snaps his fingers at me, the way you would a dog, and I obediently stand. He places his hand on top of my head and squeezes, just enough to look gentle to anyone watching, but forceful enough to make my head ache. I *have to concentrate on not rubbing my temples or begging him to stop.*

"I guess me and my family will be going then."

Mrs. Seton stands with a frown on her face, and she looks at me. For a moment, I wonder if she is going to ask me if I'm okay. And I'm shocked when I realize I would tell her no.

But instead of a conversation without words, she lowers her head, as if she's unwilling to be a part of this. It is in this moment I realize I can't trust or rely on anyone but myself. If I don't look out for me, who will?

While we turned to walk out of the principal's office, I wanted to beg someone to please stop us. Please, anything to prolong what is going to happen the moment we step foot in the house. If only someone had stopped us or said something, maybe I wouldn't have ended up in the hospital later that evening. My father, once again, told his fairytales to the adults who wished the problem would just go away.

****

I stare at Brenda, lying in her hospital bed. She looks so peaceful in her sleep. Her auburn hair is spread out on her pillow, framing her head, almost like she has a halo. I stand and wipe a few hairs away from her forehead, and she murmurs and turns her head, blocking my sight of her beauty.

I can stand here like this forever and always be content. I've gone from always being restless to being grounded, all because of her. But why? I can't consider anything with her. The most I could offer her is a good fuck, and she deserves more than that. So much more.

God, I'm tired, so very tired. I need to sleep but I can't. Sir awaits me in my dreams. But now here lately, he stands in front of me when I'm wide awake, and I'm reduced to that fucking sniveling kid who always cowered in a corner, begging not to be hit again. The more I begged, the harder the strikes would come each time. He always said he hated tears, but if he did, why wouldn't he stop when they were shed?

The room is suddenly out of focus, and I'm freefalling through an abyss and into darkness. I grip the bed railing to stop my descent, only to pull it into the darkness with me.

"Magnum."

I feel hands on my arms, and I want to push the person away...but if it's Sir, he'll hit me.

"Magnum, stop. Please stop."

I open my eyes and see the fear in Brenda's face, and I want to fall over in pain. I'm in pain because I don't know how can I save her when I can't save myself. But then I see Sir, standing on the other side of her bed, and I let out a guttural growl stemming from all the years of abuse and bottled up anger and hatred. I cover her from his eventual fists.

"Hit me, not her. I'll take her punishment," I yell to Sir. He only snarls and cracks his knuckles. I brace myself for impact.

Something soft knocks me in my head, and I wake with a start. A pillow lays at my feet, and Brenda is smiling at me. I look at her, then back down at the pillow. *Did she just throw a pillow at me?*

"You were snoring."

I must've fallen asleep in the damn chair last night. I try to roll the kinks out, but it only tightens up more.

"Shit. Sorry about that." My voice is deep and groggy.

She's sitting up in her bed with her breakfast tray in her lap. For a person who was in a serious car accident yesterday, she looks like she could star in a porno. She has that 'just fucked' hair, or I guess some would say bedhead. Shit, she even makes that damn hospital gown look good. "It's okay. I figured you needed that rest after babysitting me the past few days."

I stand and stretch with a loud yawn. "Well, I did offer to sleep in your bed, but you, as I recall, were less than enthused by the idea." I pick up her container of milk, silently asking if she's going to drink it. She gestures for me to go ahead, and I drink it in one guzzle. I crush the container and toss it in the trashcan next to her bed.

"Not going to happen. You had your chance and lost it, buddy."

I laugh out loud and instantly shut my trap when I got a whiff of the offending odor coming from my mouth. Damn, I think my eyes just watered.

"Did they give you toothpaste and toothbrush?" I walk towards the bathroom before I embarrass myself.

"I guess," she says, in between bites of her toast.

I glance at my reflection in the bathroom mirror, and I look like fucking hell warmed over. Lifting my arms, I do the sniff test, thankful that my Axe Black Chill deodorant has held up. I quickly brush my teeth, then notice the shower.

"Yo, gonna take a quick shower," I yell out before I close the door.

When I emerge, I feel more like myself, or at least some semblance of that person, whoever he is. I open the door to the sight of the doctor signing some paperwork before leaving.

Brenda holds up the papers in victory. "All clear!" she beams, and she looks radiant.

"Good, I hate hospitals."

She frowns and I feel like an asshole.

"Sorry, I didn't mind being here with you. It's just that..."

She shrugs. "It's okay. You don't owe me any explanations." She walks past me and slams the bathroom door behind her. I wince and slap myself upside the head.

"Way to go, Magnum," I mutter to myself as the showers sprays turn on in the background.

Chapter 10
Just an Illusion ~ Imagination

Brenda

I've never been so embarrassed in my life than when I had to be taken downstairs in a wheelchair, in order to be released from the hospital. I'm not used to being the passenger; I'm always the driver. Magnum further added to my embarrassment when he refused to let me stand. He, instead, lifted all one-hundred and thirty pounds of me and placed me in his car, like I was a newborn babe. Even going as far as buckling me in. I knew he was doing this for show because he winked at me as the nurse gushed at what an incredible boyfriend I had. When I opened my mouth to disagree, he slammed his mouth onto mine, ultimately rocking my world with a kiss. A *kiss*. Did I mention, with a kiss?

I wish I could say I tried to resist, but then I would be lying. Never did I realize how hungry I was for this. I rub my hands over his bald head as I inhale his scent. He smells of hospital soap and tastes like minty toothpaste. I moan into his mouth and pull him in deeper, as he unclasps my seatbelt and wraps his strong arms around my waist.

"Umm, you just need to sign this last form for me." I'm pretty sure that's what the nurse says, but I'm not paying much attention. "Ugh, please?" She taps on the car window, and I want to tell her to go away and then hang a 'do not disturb' sign on his ass.

He pulls away from our kiss, and I make fish lips, probably looking needy, but I prefer to think I looked sexy. Who am I kidding; no one looks sexy making fish lips. *Geez, Bren, desperate much?* He chuckles and takes a quick nip of my bottom lip, but moves away too quickly for me to get one last taste of him. Now I'm panting, he's got a noticeable bulge in his jeans, and my nurse is blushing. Our eyes connect, and I don't know...something unspoken passes between us. Something that is unattainable, and it scares, yet excites me.

Magnum takes the paperwork from our audience and signs it, to my surprise, he signs 'Carl Miller'. I sit back in my seat, as if in a daze. How the hell did I just make out with this man and not realize that Magnum wasn't his real name? He hands the pen and paper back to her and gives her a playful wink. She blushes again and scurries off with my wheelchair, back inside the hospital.

He closes my door and walks over to the driver's side and gets in. Leaning across, he gives me another quick nip and starts the car.

The fog from my kissed-soaked haze slowly lifts as he drives further away from the hospital.

"Cyma and Anaya wanted to be here when they released you, but I told them I got you and not to worry."

I decide to test the waters with my newfound information about him. "No problem, Carl." I peek at him from the corner of my eyes, waiting for his expression to change. To my chagrin, it doesn't, and he goes on as if he didn't hear me.

"You should probably give them a call now, or you can wait till we get to your house. I also spoke to the cops on your behalf last night about the accident. They'll probably stop by later this week for you to read and sign the necessary paperwork." He glances over at me and smiles, his lip ring still glistening from our kiss. "Oh, and I contacted your insurance company for you. They have the car and will get back to you about the repair."

My head spins with the plethora of information he just threw at me, and I couldn't get one reaction from calling him by his government name. I decide to try my luck again. "Why, Carl, you'll make someone a good wife yet."

His jaw muscles bulge, and his fists tighten on the steering wheel. Sensing he might just drive us off the road, and I've already had my fair share of accidents to last me a lifetime, I quickly explain. "I saw the paper when you signed it back at the hospital." The only sound in the car is the radio playing one of the latest hip-hop songs. I'm thankful because it lessens the awkward silence. "You never told me your real name. I love that name...Carl. Or should I call you Mr. Miller?" I steal a glance at him, and it's like this invisible wall came up.

How did we go from his hands are all over me to this?

Okay, time to change tactics. I turn up the volume and bop my head to the beat of the song. "I love this song. It's my favorite," I yell above the bass.

His lips are moving, but I can't hear him. Finally, I lean in and turn down the music. "Sorry, I didn't hear you. What did you say?"

85

"Don't ever call me that name again." His voice is calm and steady, but he is looking every bit the opposite.

I want to question him but I realize I have no right to his personal business. So instead, I slide down in my seat and sulk like any other mature adult would. My feelings are genuinely hurt. I, for some reason, thought we shared a moment together, and he was letting me in. Was it just an illusion?

We remain like this the remainder of the forty-minute drive to my house, neither of us speaking, the kiss, well, not forgotten, at least not on my part. That's why this hurts so much. He pulls in front of my house and parks the car. Not bothering to wait for him to open the door for me, I step out and storm up my steps, with Magnum in tow behind me.

"Let me get the door for you."

I refuse to turn around and show him my unshed tears. "I got it. You can go home. Thank you for everything." I open my door and walk through it, hoping to slam the door on that chapter, and his face. I quickly punch in the code to disarm the alarm.

"Bren?"

I spin around to face him. My tears of sadness are now tears of anger. "Don't you call me that. If I don't have the right to call you by your name, you don't get to call me by mine." Not exactly the strongest argument I've come up with, but it's the best I've got. Besides, I have a minor concussion; I can't be expected to come up with witty comebacks so quickly.

That invisible wall that was up in the car comes crashing around us. His expression is pained, as if I slapped him. "You don't understand." He lowers his head, and I watch his chest rise and fall, counting the seconds in between.

I'm not sure what comes over me, but I say something I swore I wouldn't bring up to him...ever. "You talked in your sleep last night."

His head snaps up, and his eyes widen. I decide to look away because if I stare into his eyes, I won't be able to finish what I set out to say.

"You spoke about Sir, and you were begging him not to hit you."

His expression goes blank, like he's been transported somewhere. I know he's standing in front of me, but he isn't really here.

"Magnum, do you carry your father's name? Is that the reason why you don't want me to say it? What did he do to you?" I take a step towards him, and he takes a step back. He lifts his fists, and I flinch, realizing too late that he's directing it to himself. He unleashes a fury of punches to his temples. I grab his wrists, but he's too strong for me. Each time he raises his fists, he lifts me an inch or two off the ground.

"Magnum, stop. MAGNUM, PLEASE YOU HAVE TO STOP!" I scream, as salty tears fall into my mouth. "Please." *Gasp*. "Please." *Gasp*.

It isn't until I fall into a crumpled heap at his feet that he finally stops, aware of my presence. He kneels in front of me, his eyes wide in horror, back with me in the present.

"What have I done?" He strokes the side of my face. "What have I done to you?" Magnum hangs his head in shame, and rakes his hands over the back of his head. His tribal tats move like a snake.

I touch his cheek. "I fell, that's all. You didn't do anything to me." I brush my fingers over his reddened temples, and lean in to kiss first his right temple, and then his left. He collapses onto my shoulder and cries. I hold him in my arms, and we stay like this until his sobs turn quiet.

My God, what did his father do to him?

Chapter 11
Make Me Better ~ Fabolous feat. Ne-Yo

Brenda

The sun shines through my Venetian blinds, warming my skin. I remove my extra firm pillow from my face, only to be fully woken by the smell of bacon and coffee. *Yum.* My stomach growls angrily, announcing it's awake as well. I stretch languorously in my bed. What was that sound? Was that my bones cracking?

It suddenly dawns on me; how did I get in my bed? Then the memory of yesterday falls on me like a ton of bricks. It was yesterday, wasn't it? I called Magnum, Carl, and he…he…oh, my God, I'm the reason why he broke down in the vestibule. I caused him pain, all because I had a bruised ego. I'm a piece of shit. A queasy feeling hits me, and I suddenly lose my appetite for breakfast.

Had I known he would have that type of reaction, I wouldn't have said anything. Magnum has been incredible with me, and I'm the worst friend in the world. But what the hell did his father do to him? It's obvious he was abused by him, but where was his mother? Was she abused as well? So many questions are running through my head, it's making me dizzy. I kick my legs over the side of my bed and walk to my bathroom to splash some cold water on my face.

Walking out while towel drying, I feel wide awake and still ashamed of my behavior yesterday. "Apologize, that's what I'll do." I say the words out loud.

"Sure, but after breakfast." Magnum's voice startles me, and I drop the towel to the floor. I look around as I bend down to pick up the damp cloth.

"My goodness. You scared the hell out of me." I clutch my hand that is holding the towel to my chest.

He rises from my bed and saunters over to me in nothing but his jeans. No shirt; just this man, in front of me and with...*wow*, no shirt. I might be hypnotized by his pecs as they flex with every movement. If I concentrate hard enough, I'm pretty sure they're saying, "Come to me, come to me."

He holds his hand out, waiting for me to take it. I hesitate for a moment, biting my bottom lip as I try to figure out the right words to say to him.

"Magnum." I look down at my feet before looking back up at him. "About yesterday..."

He shakes his head. "No need. I'm the one who should apologize to you."

"But-"

"Nothing to apologize for." He tilts his head towards the door. "Come on, breakfast is getting cold."

"Shouldn't we talk about it?"

"Nothing to talk about, Mooi. Let's eat, I'm starved."

Mooi? "What does Mooi mean?"

Edging his way closer to me, his body heat bounces off him and surrounds me. Or maybe it's the other way around. He takes his hand and caresses the back of my neck. I lean into his touch, my hair falling down my back, tickling my already sensitive skin. Drawing me closer to him, his eyes never waver from my own.

"Beautiful." He kisses my forehead the way you would kiss a newborn's head; gently, not wanting to wake the sleeping baby.

But I'm awake. My body is awake from whatever fire he has ignited in me. Is it possible to combust from touch alone? Or from a simple word like 'beautiful'? How did one word suddenly come to mean so much? I would happily beg to hear it pass through his lips one more time.

He lets me go, and I ache for that touch. So much so, I almost implore him to come back to me. He walks to the door and waits for me to pass through first, but I'm too busy catching flies in my mouth.

Slowly, I move one foot in front of the other, as if I were walking on the moon, and gravity has escaped me. I pause at the door and stare at the body art on his chest. I *really* want to trace my tongue over the twists and curves of those lines.

"Food is going to get cold. Time for me to take care of you."

But who's going to take care of him? *Can I be that someone?*

He gives me a playful pat on the butt, shaking me out of my hallucinations of the possibility of there ever being a me and him. He closed that door a few times already, and I'm not venturing near that threshold again.

"Good. I'm starved." I chuckle nervously as I walk out of the room and down the steps. His heavy footfalls on the wood echoes through the house. I pause momentarily at the spot on the floor where we both laid together yesterday, and again, I want to apologize. As if this spot didn't serve as a reminder to him as it did with me, he walks past it and down the hall into the kitchen.

I follow behind and take seat at my oversized island.

He places my plate in front of me, complete with bacon, eggs, pancakes and sliced bananas, and I inhale deeply. *Mmm.* "This looks delicious. I didn't realize you could cook."

"My mother taught me," he says, in between bites of pancake.

I play around with my food, not wanting to scare him off with this conversation. "Really? Close with your mom?" I sneak a peek at him through my eyelashes.

He places his fork down on his plate and drinks some of his orange juice. Wiping his mouth, he belches and excuses himself. "Close enough, I guess." He goes back to stabbing his fork into his pancakes.

"It's just, it sounds so sweet that your mom taught you how to cook."

He shrugs. "It was rare when she taught me things that Sir considered 'women's work'," he replies, using air quotes.

Women's work? I bristle at his explanation of Sir's words. "Oh. So, Sir didn't mind her showing you?"

"He wasn't around when she did. It was our little secret. It was usually when he had to do his two weeks in the reserves."

"That's great, that he was in the reserves."

Magnum's fork drops to his plate, and he stills, or maybe it was the air around us. "Was it? He got passed over and passed over for every promotion in the Army. Only got out because he saw what everyone else always saw in him. He's a fucking loser, a nobody. He clung to the Army, his only claim to fame, the best way he could. Through the reserves. It had nothing to do with him wanting to serve his country. It had *everything* to do with serving his ego," he spits out angrily. He places his elbows on the counter and rubs his hands against his scalp. "Shit. I'm sorry."

"No. It's me who should apologize. Again. I can see you're in pain and I guess I just want to help."

For a moment, his eyes soften when he looks at me. "How can you help a man who is forever bonded to the chains of his past?"

Chapter 12
Ride Wit Me ~ T.I.

Magnum

"Magnum, everyone can heal from the wounds of their past." Brenda's eyes widen, both of her hands placed on top of the counter.

"Really? And what about you?" I snap. I've heard this same statement from a therapist, after several thousands of dollars.

She points to herself. "Me?"

"Yes, you. "

"I don't know what you're talking about," she accuses.

"Fine. You want to play it that way, while pumping me for information? You want me to get in touch with the feelings of my past? How about you do the same. You should be honest to yourself. At least I am." I rise with my plate in my hand, no longer having the appetite for food, or this conversation. I scrape the remainder of what should've been a nice breakfast into the garbage.

My back is to her, and I wait for something to be thrown at my head. It wouldn't be the first or the last. But it would be the first time I would care. No inanimate objects are thrown my way, so I turn to face cold eyes that used to be warm.

"Don't you take things out on me, Magnum. I understand if you don't want to talk about your past, but don't you take your shit out on me."

This should be where I say fuck it and leave. But the problem is, I'm afraid to walk out the fucking door because I'll lose her, and that's not an option.

"I'm-"

She holds her hand out, shaking her head. "It's you who isn't honest. You're too busy trying to play the tough guy that you refuse to slow down and acknowledge that you were hurt by your father."

Oh, this shit again. "Acknowledge? I'll show you acknowledge." I storm over to her, ready to bare all my scars to her. My wounds, they aren't healed; they *never fucking heal*. I stand in front of her, and she pushes away from the counter with a 'fight or flight' look in her eyes. I know that look; I've worn it a few times when my father was kicking the shit out of me.

I bend my head and grab her wrist. "Want to touch it?"

"Wh-what?"

"Come on, Mooi." I call her the Dutch word for beautiful, something I've longed to call her since the moment I set eyes on her. But I've always wanted it to be used during intimate moments between us, like the one upstairs. Not now, with the memory of Sir dirtying it. But what else would I call the most beautiful woman I've ever laid eyes on? "Touch it, you know you want to." I look at her for a pregnant moment, while she contemplates this decision. Maybe I should be the one to take longer in this decision, because once she touches it, there's no turning back. She nods her head and reaches out a trembling hand to my head. Her fingers trace along the lines of my tribal art, and she gasps audibly, snatching her hand back and touching her lips.

I lean my hands on either side of her. "You wanted to know the story behind the art, right? Those indentations are a result of a metal belt buckle repeatedly slammed into my skull."

"Oh, my God." Tears fall down her precious cheeks. I want to wipe them away, but I have to finish this.

I remember when I was a kid, when Sir was away, my mother would read me bedtime stories. I used to get caught up in the world of the stories she told, and it wasn't till later I realized that the stories depended on the storyteller. If the storyteller expresses emotions in every scene, the listener will react. So, I strip away the emotions and tell my story as if I were reading The *Wall Street Journal*. "I forgot to put away my baseball mitt. Left it outside in the rain. Sir decided to get creative with this beating, to help me remember the next time. He came home from work and found the glove laying in the grass in our yard. He picked it up and went on inside. Mom and I greeted him in the living room as we were instructed to always do." I hold up one finger. "Notice I said 'instructed' 'cause that's what he did. Instruct." I grit my teeth together as I recall the memory.

"He kissed Mom and patted me on top of my head, handing me my baseball glove and said, 'You left this outside, sport.'" He'd smiled, as if all of this were our sense of normal. But the three of us *knew* it was those unspoken words yet, why speak when you can use fists. It became that thing we hid from outsiders. It was like we were members of a club with only us three, hiding our dirty little secret. "I knew what was coming. I just didn't know when." I can't face her for the rest. I face the

96

wall, and stare at her calendar of lighthouses, wishing I could mentally transport myself there on the coasts of Maine, rather than be here, telling this story. "We finished dinner and watched TV as a family. Mom tucked me into bed, but I couldn't sleep. Because I knew." *I knew.* I take in a deep breath.

"It wasn't until three in the morning, when I finally drifted off to sleep that he entered my room. His belt wrapped around his fists with the buckle at his knuckles. I woke to punches being thrown at my head. Couldn't tell you how many because I blacked out. When I came to a few days later, I was in my room, my mother caring for me. You see, they couldn't take me to the hospital for fear of the police getting involved." I finally turn back to face her, and her hands are covering her face as she sobs silently.

"You know what excuse they gave my school for me being out for two weeks? Chickenpox. If the school had actually checked their records, they would've seen that I apparently had chickenpox twelve times. So that's the story behind the tat...it's to cover the scars." Even though she isn't looking at me, I point to each of my tattoos. "Each one of them is covering a scar; a constant reminder, courtesy of Sir."

We stand in silence for what seems like forever, or one hundred breaths. That's what it took for Brenda to be able to talk. "Magnum, I'm so sorry," she whispers.

"I've long ago acknowledged my past. I give it the respect it deserves. *None.* When I chose not to talk or think about it, it's not that I'm trying to be a tough guy. It's because I know that I'm not."

"Magnum, I didn't mean..."

97

"You meant what you said." I cup her chin in my hand, and her beautiful brown eyes look into mine. "Mooi, you and I will never lie to each other." She tries to turn her head, but I stop her because her next words would be untrue. "No more lies."

"But I'm —"

"But you are about to lie to me and say that you aren't hiding from something from your past. I've met a lot of women, Mooi. Most of whom I've fucked; they came in all shapes, sizes, or whatever. The only time I ever heard a woman say that she was just looking for a good time, no strings attached, is the tramp." I step back and look at her, shaking my head. I take her left hand and kiss her ring finger. "Mooi, you are wifey material, not a tramp. Or a woman says that because she's scared of a relationship. I'm not a rocket scientist, but someone sent you dead roses. Me, I prefer to send a lady the live variety."

Her bottom lip trembles and she wipes a tear from her face.

"You're with me, but then you're not. You pry but don't give. Someone is after you. I don't know who it is but I do know I'm here now. You're not doing this shit alone."

She lowers her eyes and places her hands in her lap. "I'm not ready to talk about it."

I kiss the top of her head. "Mooi, I'm here when you're ready." I begin to clean up the kitchen as she sits in silence. When I finish, I turn and look at her. "Get ready. We're going for a ride."

Chapter 13
Darlin' Darlin' Baby (Sweet, Tender, Love) ~ The O'Jays

Brenda

I'm sitting in Magnum's car, waiting for him to lock up my house. He refuses to tell me where we're going and honestly, I hope it isn't somewhere emotional. I don't think I can handle any more of that today. My mind drifts back to his admission to what his father has done to him, and in some way, I still have so many questions. He is also right about me having my own fair share of secrets that I'm not ready to share. So that means I have no right to question him about his past when I haven't exactly come to grips with my own. Right?

"Ready, Mooi?" He grins at me as he starts his car.

I lean back in my leather seat and close my eyes. "Mmmhmm."

"Good." He pulls off so fast it causes me to fall forward and the seatbelt snaps me backwards.

"Ouch."

"Sorry 'bout that."

We leave Queens and jump on the Long Island Expressway. What the hell is in Long Island? Apple picking? Perhaps a wine tasting? I look over at him and decide not to ask him again and just enjoy the ride. Two hours later, I'm more than ready to get out of this car. Not because I don't enjoy his company, more so because I need something to keep my mind occupied.

"We're here."

I get out of the car and look around. Not much in the area. A small grocer down that way, a sign pointing towards apple picking in the other direction and this building that he parked in front of.

"Where is here?"

He doesn't answer, but instead takes my hand, and we walk inside. A burly older man sits behind a counter and asks us to fill out some forms, and for our IDs. I look hesitantly at Magnum before handing over my driver's license.

"I'll fill out the forms for you," he murmurs.

I take the time to walk around and look in the small waiting area. The walls are wood-paneled and have pictures of various people posing with either a shotgun or other forms of guns.

"Mooi, they're ready for us."

I turn around, too quickly that I stumble, and Magnum reaches out to steady me, and perhaps saving me from twisting an ankle.

"Thank you," I say against his chest. He holds me tight to him, neither of us wanting to let go.

"I'll always be here, Mooi."

Him calling me my new nickname reaches me in the depths of my soul. I'm falling for this man in what could become a collision course.

"You two ready? We have the range set up for you."

"Range?" I question.

"Going to teach you how to shoot a gun. Need to know that you're safe when I'm not around."

"Magnum, I can't do that. Didn't you say I could just point the gun and the person would most likely leave me alone?"

"I also said that I would teach you how to use one."

"I'm not sure about this." I lower my head.

Stroking my hair, he says, "It would give me peace of mind, knowing that you knew how to fire a gun the right way."

I swore to myself I would never fire a gun. People with guns ask for violence to be brought to them, at least in my experience. I've had enough violence in my past to last a lifetime. But maybe he's right. Perhaps I should learn.

"Fine, I'll do it." I exhale a breath I didn't know I was holding.

"Thank you." He kisses my forehead and takes my hand leading me through the door the clerk is holding open for us.

****

Hours later, we drive back to my house, and I'm all but bouncing in my seat. I can't believe how exhilarating shooting that gun was for me. I could've stayed for hours, but Magnum didn't want to overtax my body since I just came out of the hospital. I insisted that I felt fine, but he wouldn't hear it.

"Can we go back tomorrow?"

He smiles at me and shakes his head. "Don't think so. Let's give you a few more days of rest before we do it again. Besides, I didn't originally plan to take you there today anyway. If it wasn't for our ...uh...convo this morning, I would've waited another week or so."

He parks the car a few houses down from mine, and we walk down the block. I see David standing in front of my steps with Finster.

"Oh hey, David. What's up?" I ask, as I jog towards him and he meets me halfway. Fin tries to run up to me, but his leash is preventing him from going but so far.

David turns and waves to me. "Hey, I was out walking Fin and saw your visitor. Told him that I saw you leave a few hours ago but didn't know when you were coming back. I guess that doesn't matter now, since you're here."

Visitor? Magnum walks beside me and wraps his hand around my waist. "You expecting someone?"

"No. But whoever it is it can't be anyone scary. Its broad daylight."

The three of us walk towards my house, and I stop in my tracks.

"Stew?"

Chapter 14
Ex-Factor ~ Lauryn Hill

Magnum

Stew? What the...?

Brenda pulls away from me and runs to this man who looks like he's in his mid to late forties. They hug each other, and I feel the urge to mark my territory. I clench my jaw so tightly I'm afraid my teeth will shatter. Who the fuck is he to her?

She unlocks the door, and the two of them go inside while I stay behind with the nerd and his mutt.

"Looks like she forgot about you." The nerd speaks, and I wonder why I didn't put a bigger ass beating on him before. Perhaps break his jaw; that way, he wouldn't be having this conversation with me now.

"Who me?" I give him a menacing smile. "I'm unforgettable, but you, on the other hand...hmm. I barely remember your name." I push past him and bound up the steps and into the house, closing the door behind me.

Brenda and this Stew person are sitting on her couch, knees touching. Where she was happy just moments ago with me, she's crying now with him.

"Mooi?"

Stunned, she looks up with red-rimmed eyes, and without thinking, my feet carry me toward her. Lifting her off the couch, I hold her to me, where she belongs.

"What the fuck did you do to her?"

Soon to be dead man Stew stands up with concern in his eyes. "No, it's not the way it looks."

"Really? She was fine when she walked in here with you a few seconds ago, and now she's crying."

"Mag, it's not Stew's fault." She sniffles.

Now I'm really confused. I look at her and wait for her to continue, when she pulls out of my grasp and takes a seat next to no longer dead man walking Stew, and pats the empty space next to her.

"Mag, there's some things from my past that you were right about." She looks down at her lap and wrings her hands together. "I didn't want to talk about the things from my past because they were horrible and so long ago that I'd rather forget them."

Stew places a hand tenderly on her knee, and I want to snatch it right out of its socket.

"I guess I should start with introductions. Stew, this is Magnum. Magnum, this is Stew."

He holds his hand out for me to shake. Perfect, this asshole has manners. Well, unfortunately for him, I don't. Stew, realizing I won't shake his hand, pulls it back, and places it on his own goddamn knee.

"It's nice to meet you, Magnum. I'm glad that Brenda has found someone."

My eyes narrow. "Yeah, I'm that someone who would kill for her."

He nods. "I see. I'm Detective Stewart Walsh."

Detective? I look at Brenda for further clarification.

"Stewart was the detective on my case."

What the fuck is going on here? "Case?" I'm too lost for words right now to add anything further.

"About ten years ago, after I broke up with my then-boyfriend, he began stalking me. Strange things would happen, like breaking into my apartment, changing the screensaver on my laptop. And..." She looks at Stew before turning to look at me. "Then it got violent. Slashing of my tires and sending me dead roses. Stew was the one who arrested him."

Dead roses? I perk up at this. "So, he's out of prison and doing this shit to you all over again?" I look over at Stew. "You're the fucking police, why haven't you picked the son of a bitch up and thrown him back in jail?"

"I can't do that."

"Why the fuck not?"

"Because he's dead, Mag."

At first, anger hits me because I won't have the pleasure of killing him myself, but then it dawns on me. *Shit.* "Copycat?"

Stew nods. "Looks like."

"But how?" I sit back into the couch, still stunned by this information bomb she dropped on me.

"That's something I'll check out. He was stabbed to death in prison five years ago. I'll take a look into who were his prison friends, and his cellmate."

"Magnum, there's more." Her gaze is unsteady.

More? What the fuck? I wait for her to proceed.

Clearing her throat, she begins, "He had a plot to kidnap and kill me, but he was apprehended before he was able to."

"Okay, well that's good news."

She shakes her head. "Stew theorized if this person truly is a copycat, then they'll be trying to carry out the final plan of my ex."

I look over at Stew, and the worry is evident. "Mooi, when is the anniversary of what would've been the kidnapping?" I have a sinking feeling that it's soon.

"Two weeks."

Chapter 15
Jump into the Fire ~ Harry Nilsson

Brenda

"Two fucking weeks?" Magnum is pacing the floor back and forth as I sit in silence.

"Brenda, I should get going. I'll give you a call the day after tomorrow with what I'm able to find."

I rise and walk with Stew towards the door, walking past Magnum, who is on the phone with Tick, most likely.

"Thank you for coming."

"I'm sorry I didn't get here faster. I was out of town on a case, so I didn't get the message." He looks over my shoulder. "But I see that you're in good hands, kiddo." He gives me a hug and leaves.

David is walking past our house with Fin. He stops to say bye to Stew and then walks up the steps.

Fin runs inside the house, barking up a storm.

"Your guest is leaving already?" David asks, as he follows me inside.

"Yes, he had to get back to work."

David stops short of the living room.

"It's okay, you can come in. Have a seat."

He looks tentatively at Magnum but comes in and sits on the couch.

"Yes, someone is out to kill her. I'm getting her the fuck out of here tonight."

David whips his head towards me. "Someone's t-trying to kill you?"

"I don't know." My voice has zero energy in it; I feel overwhelmed and defeated.

Magnum ends his call and looks at David. "What the fuck are you doing here?"

David stands to leave, but I hold his arm. "David is always welcome in my house."

Magnum grumbles under his breath.

"Where will you be going?" David sits back down.

"I, ugh...I don't know." I look over at Magnum, who is back on his phone again.

"Yeah, I'll be there later this evening. Air it out and make sure the fridge is stocked," he barks orders into his phone. Heaven help the person who doesn't obey him. He looks over at me and whispers, "You better get the guest room ready. I'm bringing company."

I know there is a strong possibility that a crazed person is trying to kill me, but my heart sinks, knowing he's putting me in the guest room. I thought, well I don't know what I thought, but I sure as hell wasn't considering the guest room.

He places his cell back in his pocket. "Mooi, you better pack some things."

"But *where* are you taking me?"

"My place," he says matter-of-factly, as he bends to pet Fin.

I know he has a place in Manhattan; he bought Tick's penthouse when he moved to Westchester with Cyma. "In the city?"

"No. My hunting cabin just outside of Little Falls."

Little who? I'm a city girl; anything north of that, I'm lost. Visions of a log cabin with no indoor plumbing and an outhouse pop into my head. "Why don't we just stay at your place in the city? It would be easier for me to get to work from there."

"You're not going to work till this shit is resolved." He stands to his full height.

Now I'm standing with my hands on my hips, ready to rip him a new one. *Who the hell does he think he is giving me orders?* "Just wait one minute, Magnum. You do not have the right to boss me around." I point at him, and Fin stands in the middle of us, confused and looking from one to the other, his tongue hanging out of the side of his mouth.

He rubs his bald head in frustration, making his appearance more menacing, yet sexy at the same time. "Mooi, I'm trying to save your life."

"Mooi?" David asks from the sidelines.

"Nickname," I say absentmindedly, because Magnum just tugged at my heartstrings when he called me my new nickname in the middle of an argument. "All I'm saying is, please include me in the decisions."

He smiles, and his magnetism is pulling me in. I walk slowly over to him, and he wraps his arms around my waist. I feel the bulge in his pants, and I want him to fuck me right here in my living room.

"Now would be a good time for you to leave." For a moment, I have no clue who he is talking to because David and Fin have been long forgotten; that's how strong of a hold this man has over me. I hear the click of the door just as Magnum slams his mouth onto mine. "I'm sorry," he murmurs into my mouth.

"Hmm?" This man is an incredible kisser, and I wonder if it's because of the tongue ring. If it's this good up top, I can only imagine how it would feel licking my clit. That thought alone has me clenching my legs together as I let out a moan.

The back of my legs hit the couch, and he turns us around, lifting me in his arms as he sits on the cushions, my knees on either side of him. Never breaking our kiss, I fumble with his belt buckle. Damn, when I was in high school, I could undo a belt buckle and zip down in no time at all. Seems like I'm a little out of practice.

"Let me," he croons, and he undoes it in a second, leaving me feeling like a virgin who doesn't have a clue.

I stand and shed my own pants, leaving myself in just my lace boyshorts. Now I'm wishing I wore a sexy thong today. He helps me take off my periwinkle cable knit sweater, and instinctively, I want to cover up my less than flattering belly fat.

With my crazy hours, I never seem to have time to hit the gym, and hadn't thought much about it until now. Shit, he's either going to love my lady lumps or not. But this is me, all of me, take it or leave it.

Rising from the couch, he reaches around me and unclasps my bra. Yet another thing he seems to be proficient at. Hmm, the thought of that ruffles my feathers a bit.

I reach for his zipper, and thankfully it goes down with ease. His jeans are slightly baggy, and I love that look on him, but they would look much better on the floor. With my help and the weight of his phone, his jeans drop to the ground, and he steps out of them.

His legs are muscular, like the rest of his body. I reach my hand inside his boxer briefs to grab hold of my grand prize, and I gasp loudly as my eyes widen, and my mouth drops.

He smiles wickedly at me. "Trust me, you'll enjoy it."

I gulp. He is slightly larger than a handful, but he has a Prince Albert piercing. From the feel of it, he has one...two...three...*four* lorum piercings on the underside of his penis.

And that's about to go inside me?

"Oh, my." My thoughts spill out verbally.

"Save that for when I'm inside of you."

Cocky bastard. But I guess when you have as many cock piercings as he does, then he has probably earned the right.

I gently rub my hand up and down his shaft, careful of his piercings.

"Rougher."

"Huh?"

He places his hand on top of mine and squeezes, yanking my hand up and down. Much rougher than I was doing.

"I didn't want to hurt you."

"You can't hurt me." He kisses the tip of my nose. "You'll learn soon enough how rough I like it."

Say what? I open my mouth to ask him that very question when my cellphone rings. Damn it, worst timing.

"You should get that."

"B-but-"

"I'm not going anywhere. When you're done, turn off the phone. You're mine for the next few hours."

I stare at him longingly before I slowly turn towards my phone and its annoying ring. "Cockblocker," I murmur as I march towards it.

"Hello?" I ask into the headset.

"Brenda? Brenda Johnson?"

"This is she."

"This is Mr. Stein, from the insurance company. We have some news about your car."

"Great. How long will it take to be fixed?"

"I'm afraid this will turn into a police investigation, ma'am. The lug nuts holding your tire in place were intentionally loosened."

I drop the phone on the floor, and my glass screen cracks, along with my resolve. Magnum rushes over to me instantly.

"Mooi, what happened?"

I'm too stunned to answer. He bends and picks up the phone.

"Who is this?" he angrily spits. Long moments of silence follow before he throws my phone against the wall. He grabs my shoulders and tries desperately to snap me out of my daze. "Get packed now, we're leaving. Don't tell anyone where you're going."

I barely hear what's coming out of his mouth at this point. My lug nuts were loosened? I could've died. I could've *actually* died that day.

"Mooi, come back to me."

I blink rapidly and stare blankly at him.

"Please baby, you gotta hold it together for a little bit longer. I have to get you out of here."

The fog slowly lifts, and reality hits again. He's right; I'll have a nervous breakdown later. I turn and run up the steps to pack while Magnum takes care of a few things downstairs.

Within twenty minutes, I'm packed, and we are in Magnum's car, headed to his hunting cabin.

How did we go from hot and heavy in my living room to hot and running from Queens?

Chapter 16

Spin Spin Sugar ~ Sneaker Pimps

Magnum

We arrive at my hunting cabin five hours later. To tell you the truth, I've never hunted here a day in my life. When I bought it, the broker called it a hunting cabin and I just never stopped calling it that. Unfortunately, I rarely have time to spend here since I work in the city and, now, Amsterdam. I help Brenda out of the car; she's still shaken from the news about her tires. I go to the trunk to gather her bags, and we walk up the stone pathway leading to my front door.

She stops and turns around, as if taking in her surroundings. I have flood lighting around the house so seeing in the dark is always easy.

"This is your hunting cabin?"

"Uh, yeah." I shrug and unlock the door.

She walks in behind me and gasps. Shit, a few hours ago, she would've been gasping underneath me. I shake those thoughts out of my head.

"Mag, this is not what I expected," she says, as she walks around the living room, casually touching the furniture.

I set her bags down in the entryway and follow behind her. "What were you expecting?"

"I don't know. I guess a log cabin with an outhouse." She smiles sheepishly at me. "But this is incredible."

"Make yourself at home." I point in the direction of the kitchen. "The kitchen is that way, wood for the fireplace is underneath the window." She nods as I give her the nickel tour. "My bedroom is at the far end of the house, and your bedroom is here." I take her hand and lead her to the first bedroom. "You have your own private bathroom."

"My own bedroom?"

"Yeah, where else would I put you? The living room?" She looks down and then it dawns on me, my mistake. "Shit, Mooi. I'm sorry. I thought you would prefer your own room." I place my misunderstanding at her feet, as if I was just looking out for her privacy, not willing to admit the problem is mine alone. If we shared a room together, she would quickly notice I rarely sleep.

Pushing her chin out, I see and feel her walls building back up. And I'm on the wrong side of them! "No, you're right. I would prefer my own room. Thanks for thinking of it." She walks inside her new digs and promptly closes the door in my face.

Guess I deserved that. I slap myself upside my head. "Mooi, your bags," I call through the door but she doesn't respond. I get her bags and place them beside the door. "Your bags are here when you're ready for them." I stand there, waiting for her to open the door, or say something. Should I apologize? I guess I could try to explain it to her, but I don't think I can take the pity in her eyes.

I lean my head on her door, willing it to open. I don't like being on this side one bit. *Let me in, Mooi, please let me in.* I don't know how long I stand there, but eventually, the door cracks open a bit. I stumble but catch my footing.

"Mag? What's wrong?" Her voice is tentative.

"I can't sleep."

Her eyes soften. "Want me to make you some warm milk?"

I close my eyes and shake my head. "No. You don't understand. I see him when I sleep."

"Sir?" She says his name as if she was saying the boogeyman's name. I guess he is, isn't he.

"Yes, that's why…"

"That's why you put me in my own room?"

I nod. "I don't like this. I don't want you to shut me out." The words tumble out clumsily. It's always me who shuts everyone out, not the other way around. I don't like feeling like this with her.

She holds her hand out to me. Without hesitation, I take the lifeline, letting her guide me inside and to her bed. Climbing on the bed, she pats the empty spot next to her, and I lay down next to her. Without words, she places her chest to my back and holds me as a mother would her child. My body relaxes into her touch, and for the first time, I let my guard down. She kisses my neck and ear gently, and whispers the words I needed to hear so many years ago. "I'm here, I will protect you."

I'm not one of those men who are afraid to show their emotions. Perhaps if Sir had a way of showing his, I wouldn't have become his punching bag. So when the tears fall down my face, it feels cleansing. I cry until I do the most amazing thing. I fall asleep.

Chapter 17

Out Of My Head ~ Lupe Fiasco feat. Trey Songz

Brenda

The warmth of the sun coats my face as my eyes flicker open. I'm laying on Magnum's broad chest. I tilt my head to see the peaceful expression on his face as he sleeps. I can lay like this forever. He squeezes me gently, and a smile spreads across his face.

"Good morning," he murmurs.

I try to sit up, but he holds me in place. "You're up? Did I wake you?"

"No, been up for a while. I was just listening to you breathe." He kisses the top of my head while rubbing my shoulder.

"What? Was I snoring?" I've been told that I do snore sometimes.

"Nah, nothing like that."

"So, you were just listening to me breathe?"

"Mmmhmm. It was calming."

"How did you sleep?" I trace my fingers over the body art on his chest. I don't remember him taking off his tee last night, but honestly, what woman wouldn't be happy to lay on his bare chest?

He stretches, and I instantly miss his arms around me. Then he slaps me playfully on the butt, causing me to yelp.

"I slept better than expected."

"No nightmares?"

"No. Or at least not as bad as they were before."

I kiss his chest. "I'm so sorry. I wish I could take it all away."

"This is just some shit I need to deal with. Thank you for putting up with it. Most women would've run."

"Well, I'm not most women." I pat his chest and sit up. "It takes a lot more to scare me off." I'm a nurse on the pediatric cancer ward. If that doesn't toughen a person up, I don't know what will.

"That you are, Mooi. That you are. Why don't I make you some breakfast?" He stands and stretches again, his muscles flexing, and I swear the sunlight is hitting him in all of the right places. My eyes follow the lines of his abs down to the large erection in his sleep pants. And to think, I had a chance of that being inside me yesterday. I lick my lips, wishing they were licking any part of his anatomy instead.

"What would you like for breakfast?" he asks as he quickly checks his cell messages.

I almost replied, "You" but I catch myself in time. "Anything will do."

He places his cell back on the nightstand and kisses me quickly on the lips. "Cinnamon French toast?"

"Mmmm. You know the way to a girl's stomach." And heart. He is definitely finding his way into my heart, little by little.

"We'll have breakfast and then go to buy you a cell."

I forgot about what happened to my phone yesterday. "Yes, I do need a new phone. I also need to give Stew the update about my car."

"Go ahead and call him." He hands me his phone and walks out of the room.

I dial Stew's number by heart, but the phone goes straight to voicemail. "Hey, Stew, it's me. My phone is broken. You can reach me on Magnum's number. I'll text it to you." I hang up, leaving out what happened to my car. That didn't seem like the type of thing to leave on a voicemail message.

Without Magnum being near me, I suddenly feel out of place. I look over and see that Magnum has placed my suitcase on top of the dresser. *Fine, I'll unpack.* I walk over to the dresser and open the suitcase. Removing various items from my bag, I open some drawers and start placing them inside.

I turn to look at the oak chest behind me. I try to open the front doors, but they're locked. I stand there for a long moment, trying to figure out why would he lock them.

"Something wrong?"

I spin around to see Magnum standing by the doorway.

"Oh, no. I was putting away my clothes and wondered why these doors were locked."

121

Smiling, he walks in and lifts the small latch at the top. "There you go."

My cheeks warm. I'm an idiot. "Sorry, I didn't see the lock there."

Pulling me into his embrace, he nuzzles the top of my head. "I have nothing to hide from you, Mooi."

He is the most complicated, uncomplicated man I've ever met. Complicated because of his past but uncomplicated because he is so...so opposite of me.

He takes my hand into his own. "Come with me, I want to show you my room. I should've done that last night." I follow him down the hall to the last room in the back. He opens the door, and his room is double the size of my already too-large bedroom. His ceiling is vaulted with the exposed beams. The bed seems to be custom-made because it's definitely larger than a king. The walls are painted a mocha color, and the room has soft shades of brown and Tiffany Blue. I can almost guarantee a woman decorated this room, and I'm completely jealous.

I stroll around the room, taking in the details. "Who decorated?"

He leans on the wall, watching me. "Anaya did the decorating for the entire house."

Relief settles over me, and because my back is to him, he misses the wide smile that has spread across my face. *Good, I don't have to cut a bitch.*

"Feel free to open the drawers and look."

I turn and look at him; there is something in his eyes. "Magnum, that's too much." I don't know how I would feel if someone went looking through my stuff. But he did just give permission.

He walks over to me and takes my face in his hands. "Mooi, I want you to. I want you to see me. All of me."

"Mag, I don't understand."

He walks me over to his dresser and pulls open a drawer. "It's okay."

I stare at the open drawer and then back at him. Uncertainty hits me, and I'm not sure if I'm ready for everything he wants me to see. It's not like we're a couple or anything. But the thought of him with anyone else makes me want to scream.

I look at the open drawer, which appears to be socks. Closing it, I glance at him and he nods, giving me permission to carry on. The next drawer I open has boxer briefs. Well, I already knew that's what he wore from our almost sexcapade from yesterday. Feeling a bit braver, I close the drawer and bend to open the middle drawer. T-shirts. I finish looking through all six drawers in the dresser and move on to his nightstand.

When I open the top drawer to his nightstand, I'm shocked to see books. *Moby Dick*, and *War and Peace*, among others. Holding *Crime and Punishment* in my hand, I look at him.

He smiles deeply. "Yes, I love to read at night. For obvious reasons."

"Hmm, with a body like yours I would've thought you preferred other activities at night...of the female persuasion," I kid and place the book back in its place.

"Keep looking, you'll see."

I turn my head right and left to see where else there is to look. "Nowhere else to go from here." I shrug. "You, my dear man, lead a very boring life." I laugh out loud and try to walk past him. He places a hand on my waist and points to a corner that has a chest, one of those old antique ones with the distressed leather and travel stickers on it.

"What's in that?" I ask as I slowly walk towards it, where I stop and kneel down in front. Perhaps it's old maps or a gun collection. But somehow, I know, I just know, it's not. My hands on either side of the door, I debate if I should open it. Once I see whatever is inside, I can't unsee it.

"Mooi, don't be afraid. This too is a part of who I am. Open it."

Can I handle another surprise in my life right now? I've had quite a few in the past few weeks. But I decide to move forward and open it.

Inside the chest are at best, what I can describe as toys. BDSM toys that I've read about in some erotica books. I do a quick mental inventory of everything. Handcuffs of different varieties, whips, and floggers, and some other items I'm not too sure of their purpose.

"Y-you're into this?" I swallow down my fear. *So yesterday, this is what he would've done to me? Tied me, gagged me, and fucked me?*

He touches my shoulder from behind but I flinch, and he pulls away. Feeling like a piece of shit, I stand and turn to face him. "I'm sorry about that. It's just that you caught me off guard."

He nods, masking the pain in his eyes. "Yes, I'm into this. But I don't expect you to be."

"So you would be okay if we do normal sex?"

His eyes flash wildly. "What's normal sex, Mooi? 'Cause I sure as hell don't know what that is. Sex is sex. What may get one person off may not get the other person off. What's abnormal about that?"

"B-but, you have to admit that beating the shit out of someone to fucking come is not normal."

"Who said anything about beating someone up? I don't get off on beating anyone up, especially women. If done right, I could spank your ass just right and have you come from that alone."

My hands instantly fly to my butt and rub it as if he just laid me over his knee. "You are not spanking my ass."

He exhales loudly. "I wasn't planning on it. This would have to be consensual. If you agree, then I'm with it. If not, then it's okay. It's not a deal breaker for me."

I point to the chest in the corner. "Then why insist that I see this?"

He takes a step closer to me, and I'll be damned if my body didn't just react. Damn him.

"Because it's a part of me. I didn't want any secrets between us."

"There's an us?" I regret the words as soon as they come out of my stupid, thoughtless mouth.

His face shows the sting of my words. "Well there is definitely something between us. Can you admit that much?"

I look away from him, embarrassed by my actions, my words, just everything. "Yes, there is something there." I can't deny that. "But would you be happy with just me? I would always question, every time we had sex, if you are truly satisfied."

He strokes the side of my face. "Mooi, with you in my bed, I could just hold you all night and be content. Listening to you breathe gives me dreams, watching you gives me hope, being with you gives me life. You are, and will always be, more than enough for me."

"I'm just afraid. I don't want to fall deeper for you and realize that this isn't what you want." I point to his treasure trove of secrets. "I'm not sure where I fit in."

"You fit in wherever there is a you and I."

I try to walk away from him to get some space to think, but he holds me in place. "Mooi, no more running. We are alike in that. Always running from our past, not wanting to put roots down. It's simple; there is a you and there is a me. That's all."

My lips begin to tremble with emotion, and he kisses me, his tongue ring clicking on my teeth and sending shivers down my body. His touch is warm and incredibly soft. My fears are stripped away with this kiss, and fall to the floor, along with my clothes.

I wrap my arms around his neck as he is about to carry me to the bed, but I want him now. I don't want to wait any longer. We've waited too long, so much time has been wasted. I stop him and drop to my knees, undoing his sleep pants. My fingers grip the waistband of his briefs, but he halts me.

He turns, and I watch the skull and swords on his back move as he walks towards the chest. My heart drops. I'm not enough for him. I sit on the floor, contemplating if I should make a run for it or have a rational conversation like an adult. He rummages through the chest for a second and pulls out a box of condoms. My cheeks burn with embarrassment.

Am *I enough?*

He kneels down beside me and places the box next us on the carpet.

"We should move this to the bed," he says as he bends to kiss my neck.

"No, no more waiting, I need you now," I pant, my heartbeat racing from his tongue tracing my collarbone.

He pauses and pulls away. Standing, he removes his briefs, stepping out of them and leaving them on the floor. He lays on his back and beckons me to him. I crawl over and straddle him.

He strokes his already rock hard dick, and I watch his movements that are purposely slow. His eyes beckons for me to take over and I do. I place my hand on him, and let out a loud sigh.

He guides my hand up and down as our eyes are locked on one another, feeding each other's soul.

"You're enough for me, Mooi." His voice rumbles, like the sound of thunder in the distance. Not scary, but enchanting.

I swallow the lump in my throat as I try to allow myself to believe that I *am* enough for him.

Deep in my thoughts, I absentmindedly stroke him as I try to come to grips with what he is telling me. Precum coats my finger as I rub my thumb over his tip. He is purposefully giving me the control and allowing me to set the pace of this, trying to prove to me what his words are unable to.

I reach for the box and remove a condom. Tearing it with my teeth as if I were a starved woman, I unroll it on to his sizeable length. Licking my lips, I lift myself and slowly seat myself on his dick. His hands fly to my waist and hold me. I flinch at first at the size of him filling me, penetrating me.

"Slow," is all he says as my eyes roll to the top of my head and I slowly bring myself the rest of the way, in the most delicious pleasure imaginable, each of his piercings hitting my g-spot on the way down.

"Oh," I breathlessly say.

"Mmmm," he moans, his eyes closed. I want him to open them for me. I want to see his chocolate kiss-colored eyes.

His hands move up and down my sides and eventually land on my ass cheeks, squeezing them. I arch my back, placing one hand behind me on his thigh and the other on his chest to steady me as I move. I lift up with my knees and the help of his hands. His hands are a steady guidance and spur me on.

In each of my slow movements, I feel every inch of him, and I am savoring it. Can this last forever?

"Damn you feel so fucking good," he groans.

I'm too busy biting my bottom lip and trying not to cry from the pleasurable feeling of him inside of me. He bucks his hips, and I yelp out in pleasure. He bucks again, and I know I will come undone if he keeps this up.

He positions me in a way that I won't fall as he sits up and pulls me in to kiss me. Our tongues clash and duel with each other, each of us staking claim to the other. Pulling my mouth from his as he moves his hips in short thrusts, I bite his shoulder, marking him. He wraps one arm around my waist as his thrusts become more powerful.

A cramp is building in my legs, but I ignore it, not wanting to break this connection we have. He pulls my legs straight on either side, lessoning the pressure on me and continuously thrusts, harder and harder.

My arms dangle down his back as I find another spot to mark him.

"Mmmm," he groans, not from the pain but from the desire of it.

His strong hands clutch my sides tighter. "Look at me," he commands, and I willingly obey.

I look into the depths of his eyes, his spirit; together we are soaring past the sky and into the sun, to be burned and our ashes forming into one.

"Give it to me, Mooi."

As if I were a coil tightly wound, my resolve snaps and bounces off the walls. Sweat falls from my breasts down my stomach and joins where our bodies meet. I cry out my orgasm, my body shuddering, as if I was under a spell. His release soon follows my own with a loud groan, and I am exhilarated that I was the one who did this for him. Not his bag of tricks but me, and only me. I *am* enough. He falls back, and I collapse onto his chest, breathless and tired.

I lay on top of him until my breath steadies.

"Mag?"

"Hmm?"

"Show me what's in the chest."

Chapter 18
Voodoo ~ Godsmack

Brenda

I look at my reflection in Magnum's car mirror. Damn, I'm glowing. Between the huge smile on my face and the fact that my face looks like a spotlight is beaming down on it, I'm pretty sure people in town will know we just had incredible sex a few hours ago. I mull over the idea of sending his body piercer a thank you note. Hmm, wonder how many women ever thought to do that...or perhaps I'm not the first. I nibble on my bottom lip as I ponder this some more.

His hand reaches over and squeezes my chin. "Keep biting those pretty plump lips, Mooi, and you're looking for me to pull this car over and fuck you in the back seat." He traces his thumb over my lips, the same way he did when I laid in his arms not that long ago.

I close my eyes and feel those moments all over again, when he first made love to me and later, our frantic love making by the chest. Crossing my legs, I squeeze them together as the sensations take over. I open my mouth wider and wrap my lips around his thumb. Twirling my tongue and sucking on his thumb, he moans out loud.

"Mooi." His voice is desperate and needy, just like my willpower.

I take his thumb deeper in my mouth, but the need to have him inside of me again is too strong. As if my hand had a life of its own, it slides into my pants and inside my panties.

Inhaling through my nose, I feel the relief when my fingers open my folds. My head rolls back on to the headrest.

"Is it wet for me?"

I don't answer because I'm flying on Cloud Nine and I don't ever want to come down.

"Pretend it's me, Mooi."

My fingers thrust inside of my opening in a quickening speed. My heart beats in my ear as my skin becomes coated in sweat.

"Close?"

I moan out my answer. Words are completely escaping me, reducing my vocabulary to hums, and that's about it.

"Don't come. Save it for me."

My eyes fly open, along with my mouth. He removes his thumb and strokes my chin.

He smiles lazily. "You heard me right, Mooi. Save that all for me. I promise you I'll make it worth it."

I swallow hard, and stroke myself a few more times, debating what I should do. I've always been about instant gratification but what he is offering is so much more tempting. I remove my hand from the warmth and moisture of my opening and out of my pants, my fingers glistening from my juices.

Reaching over, he takes my hand and places those same fingers in his mouth and sucks deeply. The pull on my fingers reaches down to my stomach and even further down south. *How did he just make my toes curl?*

He turns his head and stares at me for what is only a second but feels like an eternity. So many things pass through us in that split second. Promises of pleasure beyond my wildest imagination...and something more. A bond of sorts that has tightened around us.

Releasing my fingers from his mouth, he holds my hand in his and kisses the back of it.

"We're here," he murmurs, in between kisses on my wrists.

Here? I'm confused, but then I turn and see the picturesque village.

"It's beautiful here."

He smiles. "I know. I chose this area for the tranquility and privacy." He parks the car in front of a restaurant with a sign reading, "Martha's Spoonful."

"Is the food there good?" I ask as I open the car door.

"The best fried chicken and okra I've ever had in my life." He pats his stomach.

"Should we try dinner here?" I close the car door as he comes around behind me, swatting me gently on the ass.

"We could do that. Or we could order something to go, and I eat it off of you back at the house." He wiggles his eyebrows, which looks both cute and funny at the same time with the piercings.

Wrapping my hands around his neck, I gently tug on his lip ring with my teeth. "Mmm. I think I like your idea better."

"Then it's a date." He gives me a quick nip and we start walking, hand in hand.

I look around like one of those tourists I usually make fun of in the city. The town is nestled in between the mountains. This is what I would call a Kodak moment.

"Here's the cell phone place." He stops in front of another store front with a burgundy awning.

Holding the door open for me, we both walk inside.

"Ahh, Mr. Magnum. What can we do for you today?" A clerk, who looks to be in his mid to late forties, comes from around the counter and shakes his hand.

"Looking for a smartphone for my girlfriend." Still holding my hand, he gives it a squeeze, just the way my heart fluttered when he called me his girlfriend.

The clerk, who's name tag reads Ted, turns to me, smiling and offering his hand to shake.

"Nice to meet you, I'm…"

"Candy. Her name is Candy. You can refer your questions over to me." Who the hell is Candy? And why is he calling me by that name? My eyes narrow at my soon to be ex-boyfriend. That's gotta be a record somewhere as the shortest romance in history clocking in at three seconds.

Ted smiles and nods before turning to the wall of phones on display.

"No real names, not till we figure out what is going on," he whispers. I lower my head to hide the reddening of my cheeks. Shit, I jumped to conclusions as usual. I really have to work on my trust issues.

Ted starts pointing out phones and rattling off everything they can do. Bored, I walk around the small store when something catches my eye.

"Umm, Mag. Is it okay if I go across the street?"

He turns to face me and frowns. "Not sure if that's a good idea."

"You can watch me from this window," I plead in a childlike voice that I haven't used since I was five.

He walks over and kisses me. "Be careful. Yell if you need me."

"Oh, I'll do more than that," I promise before I walk out of the door. I cross the street quickly - no need to look both ways in this lazy town - and turn to see him staring at me from the window. I smile and wave at him, and have to actually hold myself back from throwing him an air kiss. When did I become this 'hearts and roses' woman?

I stare at the black awning that says, "Milly's Pleasure Emporium." I guess people in small towns need to get their freak on too.

A senior couple walks past me, the old woman turning to stare and shake her head in disapproval. For a moment, I'm transported back in time to Sunday school and being caught smoking behind the church. I shake away the disappointment and open the door. A bell chimes, announcing my arrival, to pleasure or hell, depending on who you ask.

I've been inside sex toy shops before; I usually go straight to the vibrators and flavored condoms, then leave. But I wasn't quite expecting a shop like this in the middle of nowhere.

The shop has a goth look to it, with heavy metal playing in the background. I feel like I'm in a bigger city than this small village.

A woman in a red leather bustier, black leather pants that looks like they were sewn on to her, and platform shoes walks over to me. Her hair is dyed a bright purple, and she has a pot-smoking Care Bear tattoo on her neck.

"Hey there," she smiles, and the only thing I can focus on is her lipstick. What an amazing color.

She must've noticed my staring like an idiot because she points to her lips and says "Sephora, passion purple. And yep, I took this color to my guy, and he dyed my hair to match."

Breaking the ice, I burst out laughing, clutching my stomach. "It looks amazing on you."

"Thanks, you don't look like you're from around here." She smiles.

I give an exaggerated look at my outfit, and then look at her. "Really?"

She laughs some more. "Oh, I meant, I would've remembered you." She spreads her arms wide open. "Small town, ya know."

"I do. I'm just here visiting with my b-boyfriend." The last word still foreign to my lips but it tastes just right.

She winks at me. "I bet he's hot."

My cheeks warm when I think of exactly how hot he is, but before I get a chance to respond, I hear his voice.

"I'm definitely not as hot as her." His voice is raspy and turns that dull ache for him into a throb of need.

I spin around to see him staring at me as if I were the only woman in the world. I can't help the smile that spreads across my face.

"Oh, you're with Magnum?" she asks, and I instantly question if she has been with him.

My smile falls as this question swirls around my head like a tornado. The ever-perceptive Magnum catches the look on my face and shakes his head. Relief settles over me, and I realize that I would have castrated him if he did sleep with her.

"Hey Milly, I see you met my girlfriend." He walks towards us and without thinking, I instantly angle my body towards him. He is the sun, and I am orbiting around him.

"I'm Candy." I extend my hand to her, which she takes.

"Nice to meet you, Candy. You have a great guy here."

I look up at him and smile. "I know."

"So tell me, what can I do for you today?"

I lower my head, suddenly feeling embarrassed. It seemed like a good idea before he came inside. Now I'm not so sure. I peek up and see he is staring at me intently, waiting to hear what I have to say.

"I...ugh." I turn around and walk towards the vibrators. "Just uh...looking."

Magnum follows behind me. Wrapping his arms around my waist, he whispers in my ear, "Hmm, vibrators? Thought I took real good care of you earlier without one, but I'm all for it, if that's your kink."

I lean my head into his chest as butterflies swirl around in my stomach. "That you did."

"You didn't come in here for a vibrator, did you?"

I swallow hard and close my eyes, enjoying his warm breath on my skin. "No."

"I told you, whatever you want to know, you can ask me. I rather it come from me than someone else."

I turn to face him. "But there are some things I may be too embarrassed to ask you."

"I had my tongue inside you as you came in my mouth. I sucked you dry of every juice you dropped, and you feel shy about asking me questions?" He quirks an eyebrow.

"Well, I feel stupid, now that you put it that way."

He places his hands on my shoulders and gives me a gentle squeeze. "I told you before that you don't have to try it. I think I proved to you that I'm good with having sex without the extra kink."

I lower my eyes, as I come to grips with what I'm about to admit. "The thing is, I think I want to try it. We can start slow and if I like it, work our way up."

A wide smile appears on his face. "Then we can explore."

"If I don't like it, then we can stop."

"Mooi, are you sure? I don't want you to do this for me."

I shake my head. "No, it's about me."

He shrugs. "Okay, then we will explore this together. First things first, you need to pick a safe word. It has to be something that you'll remember."

I glance towards the shop window and stare at a store awning across the street, next to the cell phone store. The awning is green with white lettering and a picture of a dill pickle on it.

I turn back to Magnum and smile coyly. "Pickles."

"Pickles?" He smiles hesitantly at me.

I shrug. "Sure, why not. I love pickles in all shapes and sizes." I playfully rub my finger on his crotch.

His eyes are alight with lust as he lets out a groan. "Pickles it is, then." He grabs my hand and tugs me behind him as he walks towards the door. "Gotta get you back in bed."

I lick my lips in anticipation of the things his look promises. "Perhaps I get to test out my safe word tonight?"

He turns around and winks at me. "Only if you're a good girl."

We reach his car, and Magnum opens the car door for me. I pick up the bag that holds my new cellphone in it, as Magnum places our takeout behind my seat.

I turn around and kiss him as the same old couple from earlier walks past us. The wife once again looks at me as if I'm the biggest sinner she has ever seen in her life.

Magnum pulls me in closer for the kiss just as his phone rings. Now it's my turn to let out a groan.

He pulls away and looks at me. "Hold that thought." He reaches into his jeans pocket and answers the phone. "Mom?" He's silent for a long pregnant moment before nodding his response. She must say something else because he finally answers. "I'm on my way."

Hanging up the phone, he strokes my cheek with the back of his hand gently, soothing, but his eyes show the opposite. "We gotta go. Sir died."

Chapter 19
Ball and Chain ~ Janis Joplin

Brenda

We arrive at Magnum's childhood home in Long Island. For the better part of the five-hour drive, he remained silent, as I busied myself with reading road signs. We are still so new to each other, I'm not sure how to comfort him, or if he even wants it. Eventually, we get off the expressway and drive through tree-lined streets of normalcy. The picturesque town reminds me of a Norman Rockwell painting, capturing that part of middle Americana that we all strive for one way or another. What people often don't see in those pictures is the real story behind those white picket fences. Or perhaps we choose not to see them and prefer to think everything is forever perfect...picture perfect.

I look over at Magnum and watch his walls literally build up around him, walls that we were able to bring down, and I fear I may not be able to again. The thought of being shut out bothers me most of all. How, in such a short period of time, did I grow to depend on him? Without thinking, my hand reaches out to touch him, even if it is to feel the fabric of his clothes. I just want to feel anything that belongs to him. The car slows to a stop and before my hand makes contact with his shirt, he turns to look at me.

"This is where I grew up."

My mouth is bone dry, and my lips suddenly feel chapped. I lick my lips to moisten the dried skin. "Oh." My voice is hesitant and unsure; kind of how I feel at this very moment.

"Sorry to drag you into this shit," he mutters, his eyes trained on his childhood home, where ordinary vacated and horror began.

"Oh Mag, you're not dragging me into anything. I want to be here. Anything you need from me, I want you to know I'm here." I speak the words from my heart, and I pray that he is receiving the message.

He clears his throat before responding. "Thank you for that, Mooi." He faces me and his eyes are moist. I want to take him in my arms and make it all better, to erase the horrible memories of his childhood, and I want him to know that there is someone who cares about him. But I don't know how to express all this, except to pull him into me and kiss him.

Our lips meet, and I taste the salt from his tears. His lips tremble as our tongues dance with each other. I inhale his scent, which puts me on a beautiful ledge I am anxious to take the plunge over, into the abyss with this man. I, in return, try to give him my strength through this kiss, and I feel him give in to me. We are not just physically connected in this moment, but emotionally connected as well. If I could drink this moment and bind it to me forever, I would. But instead, I commit this to my heart and lock it away.

Slowly he pulls away from me, and I want him never to leave. *Can we stay like this forever?* His mouth glistens, and I trace my fingers over his lips. He kisses the palm of my hand, sending tingles up and down my body.

"We should get inside, Mooi." He says the words but makes no other move except to stroke my face, my neck, my hair.

I want to whine and pout because I don't want to break this moment but I give in to what is the practical thing to do. "You're right. Don't want to give the neighbors a peep show." I laugh nervously.

His eyes narrow as he smirks. Gently, he traces the contours of my face with his thumb. "Oh no, Mooi. When you and I make love, it's art; beautiful and soulful. It ought to be shared like the masterpiece it is. But I'm covetous of what you and I have, and I never want to share you with anyone. When I'm inside you…" He closes his eyes, as if savoring a not so long ago memory. "When I'm inside you, I'm laying down the foundation of the masterpiece. But when you come for me…" Slowly he opens his eyes and stares at me so intently that it rocks me down to my core. "When you come for me, I know what true beauty is, what a masterpiece should be, because it is you."

Oh. My. God. I feel like I am floating, hovering somewhere in between him and earth. But I will always gravitate towards him. "Mag, I don't know what to say." My words are clumsy because of the fog now covering my brain.

That smile of his, that I have grown to love and lust after, appears. "Nothing to say." And with that, he opens the car door, but the spell over me has yet to be broken, leaving me immobile. How am I supposed to stand if I can't feel my legs?

He opens my car door, and I turn around to see his hand out, waiting for me to take it. I hesitate though because, like him, I'm greedy and want to prolong this moment as long as I can. Once I step out of the car, reality will set in, and we will be shared with others. I don't know if I want to do that, at least not now. But I do place my hand in his, and he helps me out of the car. The spell he has over me lifts a little but still grounds me before I drift completely away.

I look down at my shabby appearance, in a black t-shirt and blue jeans. Not exactly the way one would dress when meeting their boyfriend's mother for the first time.

"You look great," he murmurs in my ear.

I playfully swat at his chest. "Oh, you're supposed to say that to me."

Taking my hand into his, he guides me towards the house. "Nah, I'm telling you the truth. You could be in a sack and still look amazing to me."

I giggle and lay my head on his shoulder just as the front door swings open. A woman who looks to be in her late fifties or early sixties stands in front of us. Her hair is gray and is in a chignon straight from the fifties. Her face has soft features, and I see a ghost of Magnum in her eyes. She is what I would call a petite woman, and you can tell when she was younger she turned a lot of heads.

Her green eyes look at her son tenderly before turning to look at me, not so tenderly.

"Mom, I would like you to meet my girlfriend, Brenda." He bends to kiss her cheek.

She looks over his shoulder at me, still taking me in. He steps back to my side again, and I hold my hand out. "Hi, I'm so sorry to meet you under these circumstances." She stares at my hand, then looks up at her son.

"I didn't realize you were bringing company. You know how your father feels about unannounced people." She turns and walks inside the house, leaving Magnum to catch the door just before it slams in our face.

He holds the door open for me to follow him into the lion's den. I really rather stay outside where I'd feel more comfortable, but I push my selfish irrationalities aside and follow him.

"Mag, perhaps I should leave." But then I realize, where would I go? I'm being stalked by some unknown person. Nowhere is safe for me. Even though I know she'd welcome me, I can't go to Cyma's house because I don't want to bring danger to her doorstep. Perhaps a hotel?

"You're staying with me. It's okay; she'll warm up to you."

"Did she ever warm up to your other girlfriends?"

He shrugs. "Never brought one home."

My eyes widen. "I'm the first girlfriend you've ever introduced to your mother?"

He nods slowly.

Oh geez, this is going to be harder than I thought. I try to think back to my teenage years when I met a guy's mother and what I did to win them over. Well, I'm not that cute perky fifteen-year-old anymore, that's for sure. I have visions of this going south, and quickly.

Magnum walks down the hall, and I slowly follow behind. I'm pretty sure this is what walking the plank feels like. His mother is seated in the living room with only the television serving as the light. The air is stale from years of cooking fried foods, and old musty furniture. There are pictures of his dad when he was in the service on the wall and pictures of his mother, but none of Magnum. I walk over to the wall and stare closely at the frozen moments in time of this family. His mother with a constant smile and his father, the opposite. I don't want to say it is a frown, per se, but it's definitely not a smile. He looks like a man who hasn't known a day of happiness.

"That is my husband, Carl Senior," his mother says from behind me. Startled, I turn to look at her. She dabs at her tears with her handkerchief. "He was an incredible man. I wish you'd had a chance to meet him. He was a loving husband and a doting father." She points to Mag and smiles.

Magnum goes stiff, and the wall that went down again for me in the car is back up and reinforced with steel this time. I take a step towards him but stop when he says, "We are not going to do this anymore. We won't put on the façade like we did for the neighbors, the teachers, the emergency room staff. When do we ever speak the truth? He's dead, but the truth is still alive."

"Don't you speak ill of him. *Don't.*"

"Don't you lie for him." His voice doesn't rise, but he sounds defeated.

"I won't stand here and listen to you slander him." Her hand clutching her handkerchief shakes in the air.

146

Magnum spins around, and storms up the steps. Moments later, I hear a door slam as if it was slammed on my heart. I hold my hand over my chest, feeling the pounding beat as it anchors me.

His mother busies herself with straightening things in the room that were already in order.

"Carl likes things a certain way. The house always has to be exact." I have a flashback of watching *The Stepford Wives* movie as she talks and straightens.

I know I shouldn't, but I can't help the words that come flying out of my mouth. "Did you know?"

Her back stiffens before she goes back to what she was doing. "Know what?" Her voice quavers and confirms what I already know.

"Did you know what your husband did to him? Did you know how he abused him?" I can't keep the accusatory tone out of my voice.

She spins around to face me, the fire she had towards Magnum gone and replaced with grief. "H-he was trying to make a man out of him. Carl was in the Army, you see. So he was teaching him the Army way."

I can tell that she doesn't believe the very lie she has been spoon-feeding people for years. "You knew, and you did nothing to stop it?"

"He was my husband. I remember better times with him. It's just, when he kept being kicked down by the world...that's when he changed."

147

I point upstairs. "But he needed you. Where were you?"

She points to the ground. "Here. I was right here. I consoled him at night. I held him and told him it would get better. I loved him."

The hairs on the back of my neck stand on end. "You weren't here for him. You were too busy pretending what was going on was normal. But you knew. You knew it wasn't normal, you knew it wasn't right. You could've taken him and ran, but you decided to stay. Why?"

"Because I loved my husband. You don't just break up a family because a member has a problem. He had a sickness, so I stayed."

"You are selfish. Magnum deserves better than you and he damn sure deserves better than that piece of shit as a father." I turn on my heel and head towards the steps to be with my man. I will slay his demons since no one else did it for him.

Chapter 20
My Joy ~ Leela James

Magnum

I'm cleaning the house when the doorbell rings downstairs. Pausing to look at the clock, I realize it's too early for my parents to return home and besides, they wouldn't need to ring the doorbell.

Ding. Dong.

Who would be here this time of the afternoon? Sir didn't mention he was expecting something or someone. I amble over to the hallway window facing the street and look out. It's my best friend, Jordan. I drop the cleaning supplies at my feet and run down the steps.

Ding. Dong.

"Coooming," I scream, as I slide towards the door in my socks. I unlock it quickly and open it.

"Hey bro, didn't see your dad's car so I figured you could come out and shoot some hoops." Jordan leans on the door frame, balancing a basketball on his hip with his arm.

He doesn't know all the details of what goes on in this house, but he does know that Sir is strict about me hanging out. I try to sneak out when I can but it's few and far between.

I shrug. "Can't. Sir gave me a list of shit to do around the house."

"Damn, man. It's your birthday, and you can't get a break for one day?"

I shake my head. "No. But thanks for asking." I turn my head and look at the living room I haven't finished cleaning yet, and turn back to him. "I better go. I still got a lot of shit to do."

"Man, thank goodness we graduate high school tomorrow. At least you have just one last summer here before you leave for college." We both were chosen for the same college, UCLA. Jordan's riding on a basketball scholarship and myself, well after my injury at the game, I didn't recuperate in time, so I received an academic scholarship. Hopefully, I can get on the team when they have midseason tryouts.

Sir was more than his fair share of pissed when I didn't make any basketball teams because of my injury. But honestly it didn't bother me; I've learned to hate the game as much as I hate him. I just want to live my life the way I choose. But first, I need to figure out what that would be. Besides, would Sir let me go so easily? This knowing feeling in the back of my head says he wouldn't. He would reach up from his grave if he was dead and pull me in with him, and I've been conditioned to go without a fight.

The darkness of my thoughts covers me like a blanket, but I feel cold. I try to shake the feeling off with a joke. "Yeah, can't wait. We get to party and bullshit." Even with the words leaving my mouth, I know it won't be like that for me. Not ever. I have a feeling Sir's reach is longer than any of us truly knows.

He begins snapping his finger and singing the Notorious B.I.G. song, "We gonna paaarty and bullshit and paaarty and bullshit." He dances to the beat in his head.

I fold over in laughter as I watch my best friend goof off. "Man, I better finish this up. I'll holla at you later."

"Aight. But tomorrow after graduation, your dad still gonna let you come out, right?"

I nod vigorously. "Yeah. Which is another reason why I need to finish up in here. Don't want to give him any reason to say no."

"Okay, cool." He gives me a pound, jumps down the four steps, and raises his hands with the basketball in a victory cheer.

I laugh and wave at him before closing the door. Turning around, I look around the living room and decide to start work again in here. Two hours later, I finish the last of dusting, and I quickly walk through to make sure I got everything before my parents come home.

Before I can head upstairs to do a check, the door unlocks, and in comes my mother and Sir. Feeling confident in the work I've done, I run up to them with a wide grin and help my mother with some of her bags.

"Thank you, CJ." My mother pats me tenderly on the cheek and walks into the kitchen.

I follow behind her when Sir says, "You clean the house like I told you?" He never asks, he just gives orders.

I turn to face him. I look him in the eye before I answer him the way I've been taught. "Yes, Sir."

Standing in front of him as still as can be, I wait for him to give me permission to leave his presence. He nods his approval eventually, after he moved a few things around to check for dust.

Spinning around with the bags in my hand, I walk to the kitchen to help my mother put things away as my father walks past us and up the stairs. Mom and I work in silence putting away various groceries. She takes a couple of T-bone steaks out of the freezer and places them in the sink to thaw for dinner.

Sir's favorite meal is T-bone steak, with creamed spinach. I hate spinach, but I'm always forced to eat it. It's even worse when it's on my birthday.

Mom walks over to me with a huge smile on her face that is usually reserved for Sir, holding an eight inch Baskin-Robbins cake. It says "Happy Birthday, CJ" written in blue edible gel.

This is the first acknowledgment from my parents that today is my birthday. Sir doesn't believe in celebrating my birthday because he said it would spoil me. So, where other kids would get gifts and parties, I usually get a long list of chores to do. But since tomorrow is my graduation, my mother begged Sir to at least get me a birthday cake.

Looks like she won, for once.

"CJ. Get up here. Now!" The words thunder from upstairs and for a moment, I think the house will fall down around us.

My mother gives me a worried look before she stares at the ceiling.

A cloak of fear grips me, and I try desperately to move my trembling legs in the direction of the staircase to hell. Because that's exactly what's waiting for me at the top.

She steps to the side, as if afraid what is about to happen to me may rub off on her as I begin my death march. I climb each step slow enough to give me time to think about what I could've done but quick enough not to anger him more. By time I reach the top step, I've come up with nothing. I did everything he asked me to do. My stomach bubbles and lurches when I walk down the hall towards the window I looked out of hours ago, and my eyes zero in on what Sir has in his hands. The dust cloth I dropped on the floor when I ran down the steps to answer the door.

He is shaking with rage as he looks at the cloth and then to me. "I asked you to do one simple thing when we left this morning, and you can't even do that."

I want to run and hide, but it will only make things worse for me. "Sir, I'm sorry. It was an accident." I can't help the crack in my voice because fear has taken over.

"And you wanted to go out after the graduation tomorrow?" His sneer is one that would make Satan take a step back.

"B-but…"

"Get. To your room. Now." He barks out the order to his obedient dog, and as much as I try to move, I don't. My feet feel rooted to the floor, and my heart drops because I know what's coming.

"No." The word didn't carry the strength of conviction, but at least I got it out.

Confusion settles over his face before quickly being replaced by anger. His eyes are now narrow slits, and his hands

153

are balled-up fists. He rolls his shoulders back, the way he does when he is getting ready to take a swing at me. Normally this would be when I flinch, or try not to. But I stand there, waiting for him. He lunges for me but I step to the side, and he goes tumbling down the steps headfirst, only to land with a loud sickening thud at the bottom landing.

A loud scream erupts from my mother before I see her kneeling beside my father, crying over him. She looks at me and, just like that, she is no longer my mother, but Sir's wife. "What did you do to him?"

I open my mouth, but nothing comes out as I stare at Sir lying motionless on the ground. Did I kill him? My God, I killed him. I run down the steps, taking them two at a time, and I don't stop. I keep running until I'm out the door and halfway across our small town, never looking back. My fear of looking back kept me from going back. That is, until he died.

A soft knock at my door breaks me away from my thoughts. I walk over and open it to see the loveliest face.

"Mag, are you okay?"

Brenda's voice is so soft, as if I was this fragile creature. Perhaps I am.

"Better now that you're here."

Her smile is tentative. She's had a rough time with my mother since we arrived a day ago. She deserves a medal for that shit, actually. "The funeral home is here, along with some people from the neighborhood."

I exhale loudly. This is it. The final stretch of that bastard's life. "I'm ready."

She reaches out and touches my arm, and I fight the urge to pull her into me. I need her more than she would ever know. I can't wait to leave here and get back to what she and I had started building.

"If you need more time, I'll tell your mother." There is power in her voice.

I shake my head. "No. I'm good, Mooi. Let's get this shit over with."

Reaching up, she rubs her hand over the side of my face. "You sure?"

I can't help it, I have to pull her closer to me and kiss her. I savor the taste of her lips like a perfectly aged steak. Tender, plump, and just right, I devour her like a starved man. She folds perfectly into my arms and takes what I give until suddenly, she pulls away. I reach for her, but her eyes search my own.

"Mag? Something is off," she whispers.

I look away and walk towards the dresser, grabbing my wallet and cell. "All good, Mooi."

"No. What aren't you telling me?" Her eyes are wide, her mouth slack.

I turn to face her and smile, hoping to reassure her. "Seriously, all good. Let's go." I reach my hand out, waiting. She stares at me for a moment longer before closing her eyes and placing her hand in mine. I guide her down the steps as I contemplate what type of future I could possibly give her.

Downstairs, we are greeted by various people from our small town and some family.

I wrap my arm around her waist and pull her soft body close to mine, partially to shield me from the people who knew what happened in this house but did nothing to help me, and the other part, simply to feel her closeness. My dick twitches with need for her, but I bury that feeling deep into the recesses of my mind, the way I wish I was deep inside of her. I can get lost in her folds and her touch. I close my eyes momentarily, fighting the urge to grab her and take her into the spare bedroom.

"Mag, they want us to head towards the family car."

I look at her in her black dress with a sweetheart neck. She picked it up yesterday when I took her to the mall. She wouldn't let me see it when she was trying it on, and it's a good thing. I would've fucked her in the dressing room.

Her hair is swept to the side of her neck and falls in a bounce of curls.

"Yeah, let's go." I take her hand and walk towards the door.

My mother is already waiting inside as I help Brenda in. Once the limo door is closed, I'm transported to that day so many years ago. I stare at the floor and only see a vision of Sir laying at the bottom of the steps, unconscious. My stomach roils and I swallow the saliva that's built up in my mouth.

I try to concentrate, but my thoughts drift from past to present with such a sickening speed it's giving me motion sickness. This is the day I've prayed for, for so long. So why don't I feel happy? Wasn't this supposed to be his day of reckoning? So how come it feels like my own? I shift in my seat and Brenda places her small hand on my knee. The warmth of her hand soothes me, but somewhere deep inside, I don't want to be calm. I'm fucking mad, and I want everyone to know it. I close my mouth tight, for fear the secrets and lies would come tumbling out. He wins again...that bastard always wins. I bet he is laughing at the pussy I've become.

My throat feels like it is squeezing the life out of me and I tug at my necktie. Loosening its grip on my windpipe and sanity, I gasp for air. A bead of sweat trickles from my temple down my cheek, finally settling on my collar, where it's swallowed whole.

"Mag? Are you okay?" Her voice is the life preserver, and I am swimming towards it, needing it to pull me out of the darkness.

I know I should say I'm fine, and not to worry about me. I should ease the worry for her and lie. But I'm sick of mendacity. My life is built on lies, but it's the truth that keeps me up at night. It's the truth that slaps me in the face each morning when I wake, if I do sleep. The truth that feeds, yet starves me. Maybe I need to live with the lies and forget about the truth. But the lies fester as the truth fights to come out. I feel like a supernova that is about to leave destruction in its wake.

"STOP THE CAR!" I scream, because the truth is banging so loudly in my eardrums I try to drown it out with my screams.

"Mag, what's wrong?" Brenda turns to face me, grabbing both of my arms.

"Please, just stop the car." I place my hands on her knees. "Please, Mooi. Make him stop the car." My voice croaks as I fight the losing battle to stay sane.

Wordlessly, she nods and taps on the window partition. "Stop the car."

"CJ? What's the meaning of this?" my mother asks. There isn't any pity in her voice or worry, just annoyance.

And that's when it hits me. The last of the lies are stripped away and fall at my feet. She wasn't the one who consoled me when Sir beat me. She was the one to remind me if I would just try harder, he wouldn't have to discipline me the way he did. I fold over as a gut-wrenching pain hits me in my stomach.

Brenda's arms wrap around my shoulders. "My God. Stop the car *now*. Or so help me, I will break these windows."

My head rests on her lap as searing tears fall down my cheeks. I no longer have the strength to speak.

Brenda's hair falls around my neck like a shield as she bends to speak into my ear. "It'll be okay. Hang on. I'll get you out of here."

I feel the car come to a stop as he pulls over to the side of the road. Reaching over me, she opens the door and gives me a nudge.

"Come on, let's get out of here," she whispers.

"CJ, this is unusual and embarrassing. Pull yourself together."

Brenda angrily turns to my mother. "Why don't you pull your head out of your *ass*. I'm getting him the hell out of this car. I wouldn't advise you try and stop me."

With a strength I never knew she had, she helps me out, and I, for a change, lean on her for support. She holds my large frame with little effort as she helps me walk.

"Breathe in and exhale out." She walks me through a breathing exercise, doing it with me.

The air is helping, and the claustrophobia is going away.

"Keep breathing, Mag, and keep leaning on me. I won't ever let you fall." Her voice gives me the strength I need.

We walk silently for hours until I realize I've led us to the cemetery. She looks at me, concern flickering in her eyes. I pat her hand and lead us in, and rain begins to fall as we walk through the open gates and up the path. On the other side, we see a tent, empty chairs, and a recently buried grave.

"That's it over there," I mumble.

She hesitates for a minute. "Are you sure you want to see the grave?"

I tilt her heart-shaped face up. "I need this. How else am I going to move forward?"

She bites her bottom lip and eventually nods her agreement. "Do you want me with you?"

"Always." I kiss her quickly on the lips before taking her hand and walking the rest of the way. Flowers surround the grave and a picture of my father in uniform sits on a stand.

She releases my hand and takes a seat. I stand over the dirt-covered grave and wonder where I begin. How do I get this off my chest? I rub the back of my head, hoping to release the tension building inside me. Eventually I turn around, and the look on Brenda's face pushes me to begin. I turn back to the grave and without thinking, the words begin to flow.

"All these years, I thought that I hated you." I remove my loosened tie from my neck and twist it around my hands. "But today in the car" - I feel dizzy with emotion - "I realize it wasn't you that I hated. I hated the things you did to me." Brenda sniffles behind me. "You made me suffer in ways that no child should ever have to endure." I tilt my head up, not sure if he is in heaven or in hell. "When I needed a strong hand to guide me, you showed me your fist." My fist tightens around the cloth material in my hand. "When I needed answers, you showed me the back of your hand. When I was starved for love, you showed me hate. When I needed you, Sir..." I take a step back, my head bent because the weight of my burdens is too heavy to carry. "When I needed you, you shut me out." The rain picks up, and the sky is angry and gray. Cracks of lightning light up the area, only to throw us back into the dull gray of the sky.

"I used to need answers about why you were the way you were. Did you not love me as your son? Or did you hate me because of the opportunities my life may have had that you no longer could. But now" - I swallow the bile that wants to come up - "I still carry the scars of my past, and I don't know if I will ever heal. I didn't turn out to be the man you wanted me to be;

I turned out to be a better one instead. I no longer need the answers to my questions. You can keep them with you because I'm breaking free of you."

I drop my tie on top of the grave, releasing the bonds of my past. Without saying a word, I turn and walk out into the pouring rain. My suit feels heavy as the water soaks the fabric.

"Magnum, wait." I hear Brenda's footfalls in the puddles.

I stop and turn to her slowly, my face baptized in tears. "I'm alright. I need to get you out of this weather." My voice is hoarse but I somehow still manage the words, my protective side coming out.

She tosses back her wet hair. "I'm fine." She tilts her head up, her mascara running down her face.

My eyes lower as I try to find the right words. "Mooi, I..."

She places her finger on my lips. "Don't say it. Don't apologize. You and I don't ever have to utter those words to each other. What we have is too deep for those words."

That's the moment when I realize that I can't live my life without her. "I love you."

She wipes a tear from her eyes. "I love you too, Magnum."

I slam my mouth onto hers and kiss her ferociously, leaving behind a bond from my past while creating a better one with her.

Chapter 21
Powerful ~ Ellie Goulding feat. Tarrus Riley

Brenda

When we arrive at the house, his mother barely speaks to us as she sits in the kitchen in silence, drinking a cup of tea. Her quiet demeanor signals a brewing storm inside of her. The house is spotless after having a repass dinner for about fifty people. Not a dish out of place, and the floor looks as if you could eat off it. I wonder to myself momentarily how she does it. Does she hide her feeling behind Mr. Clean? Wipe away those awful memories with some Pledge?

Hand in hand, Magnum and I climb the stairs to our respective bedrooms to pack what little belongings we had with us. When we reach his bedroom first, I am reluctant to let go. I'm realizing just how much I need him in my life, and I don't want to ever let go; of him, us, of any of it.

He either senses my mood, or he is feeling the same way, because he opens the door and tugs me in, locking the door behind him. I stand in the middle of his room and wait for him, casually looking around but not saying a word. Silence swaddles us like a baby blanket.

His footsteps fall behind me as he moves closer. With blind trust, I lean back into him. His strong arms wrap around my waist, and he nuzzles into my hair.

"Mooi, I need you." He murmurs the words that have so many meanings. I understand each and every one of them because I feel the same.

Slowly I turn around to face this good-looking, tattooed, heavily pierced man. His ceiling light gleams off one of the piercings on his eyebrow. Hot molten chocolate eyes gaze at me, just as mesmerized as I am. I stare at him, entranced and completely under his spell.

His large hands stroke my face so tenderly that I purr like a kitten, and close my eyes. "So soft," he whispers. My eyes flicker open to see him staring at me with something more than lust in his eyes.

I open my mouth, but he places his lips over mine. He is open and ready to receive me, and I give into him willingly. Our kiss is so intense I forget to breathe, becoming slightly dizzy from it, but his capable arms hold me up.

His hands snake around my waist and lift me up, and my heels fall off my feet with a thud. My legs are wrapped around his waist, and my sex is placed just where I can get friction when he walks. Where I expect his movements to lead us to the softness of a bed, I'm surprised when my butt cheeks are placed on something hard.

Removing my mouth from his, I look down to see he's seated me on top of the dresser. *Huh?*

He smiles coyly as he pulls open a drawer and blindly searches for something. A look of satisfaction crosses his face when he finds the object he was looking for, and pulls it out.

A necktie?

A necktie.

A *necktie...*

Oh, my.

With his free hand, he places it behind my head. "Remember your safe word?"

My eyes are wide and focused on the necktie in his other hand. My skin feels sensitive and on fire. If he touches me, will I combust into flames, only to reappear made completely whole by him?

"Mooi. Look at me, baby. Nothing will happen that you don't want."

I nod my head slowly, I know what I told him before but...am I ready?

"Safe word?"

"Ah...umm..." I search my brain, which went completely blank the moment I set eyes on the material in his hand. "Pickles?"

He smiles and kisses me. This kiss is not a slow dance but one of power; not him exerting his power over me, but him giving me the control. He pulls away and searches my eyes again.

"If things get too intense, I need you to say it."

I clear my throat. "Pickles." I'm just happy it didn't come out as a question this time.

"Good. Mooi, it's important that you stay present with me throughout all of this."

I blink rapidly, suddenly extremely present in this moment. "Huh?"

His finger tenderly strokes the side of my face again. "Meaning, you will feel varying pleasures. Some will be more intense than others. But I need you present" - he points to his head - "for all of it. I will need to know when to stop and when to do more. I will go easy on you, but I will give you enough to understand. Because we are new to each other in this, I don't want to assume you're okay when you're not."

My mouth is agape, and I nod my understanding.

"Mooi, I need the words."

Words? How is he asking me for words at this moment? But I dig deep into my brain and come up with at least one. "Yes."

"Good." He lifts me in his arms and places me on my feet.

I stand there, unsure of what to do, and my heart thumps loudly in my chest. He walks around the room, and I remain in place, as if rooted to the ground, my eyes following his every movement.

He talks as he gathers various items. He takes the chair that was in front of the desk and places it in front of me. "As you get more used to this, I will increase certain elements of play, but until then, I'll go easy."

He walks over to the dresser and grabs a brush. *What the hell?* Is he going to brush my hair? Or...or...

165

He walks back in front of me and places it on the seat of the chair; my eyes are transfixed on the wooden brush with short whiskers. "You will find this is all about building trust with one another. You, trusting that I won't hurt you more than you can handle and me, trusting that you will be honest and tell me when you can't take any more."

He walks into the bathroom, and I hear running water. Is he getting a drink? I wonder if I can ask for one too since I'm parched all of a sudden. I try calming breaths, but it's not helping. "Mooi, I need you to take off your clothes."

Clothes? Oh yes, clothes. I begin the process of taking off my garment, all the while staring at that bathroom door, my imagination running away with me. I pull my dress over my head and toss it on the bed, the action looking braver than I truly feel. My bra and panties are next, and I'm not wearing any stockings, so that was pretty easy. The stripping of my clothes feels reminiscent of stripping away a former life and entering a new one.

I'm shocked that I was able to take my clothes off without hyperventilating. I stand in the middle of Magnum's childhood room, naked. If these walls could talk, what would they say about the things he is about to do to me?

Magnum comes out of the bathroom and stops for a moment, staring at me. His eyes darken with lust, and instead of embarrassment, I'm feeling horny. I clench my legs together as he walks towards me with a dark blue hand towel he has wrung out in one hand, and a dry one in the other.

"Wh-what are those for?" I stammer.

A wicked gleam appears in his eyes, he holds up the dry towel. "One will be used as a blindfold." Then he holds the wet one up. "The other is for fun."

Fun? What kind of fun can you have with a wet towel? My mind drifts to water boarding. Oh, my God, is that part of this too?

Standing behind me, he places the dry hand towel over my eyes and around my head, clipping it together with something. I reach up and feel the terry cloth.

Am I really ready for this?

Gently, he takes one wrist and then the other, and places them behind me, tying them together with what I'm assuming is the necktie.

"I'm making this very easy for you to get out of. In case you forget your safe word, you can tug on this, and the tie will slip right off."

I'm tempted to test my restraints, but I can already feel what he is talking about. The knot feels loose and flimsy.

"Mooi, you okay?" I turn my head around in my manmade darkness towards the sound of his voice. I think it's coming from my left side, but I'm not sure.

"Uh-huh."

"Words, Mooi. When we are doing a scene, I need words from you."

What is with him and words? "Y-yes."

167

A hard slap lands on the bottom of my ass, right above my thigh. I jump and let out a yelp.

My butt stings but nothing unbearable. To my surprise, the sting travels to my lower regions in the most delightful way.

Oh, my!

"That's to help you remember." His voice is low and sensual.

My mouth forms an O, but no words come out. Shit, am I supposed to say something? I get my answer when another slap lands on my butt cheeks.

"How does it feel?"

"It hurts," I pant out.

He strokes my face with the back of his hand. "Safe word hurt?"

I shake my head and another slap. *Fuck.*

"Sorry. Not safe word hurt."

"Good." I can almost hear the smile on his face. "I won't gag you this time because I want you to be able to talk to me throughout this...and also, because I like the way your mouth feels on me."

His tongue traces my lips, and I moan like a horny bitch in heat. My head rolls back, and I feel my hair tickling my spine. A giggle escapes my lips. He rubs my ass cheeks tenderly with one hand, stroking the sore spots and with the other, he reaches down and plays with my clit.

I was already moist for him before but damn if I'm not soaking wet now. He nips at my chin and licks the side of my neck like I was his favorite flavor lollipop. He pushes one finger in my opening, and it isn't enough to give me what I need. It's just a tease at this point. A frustrating one.

He adds another finger, as he cleverly moves them inside and out and around, hitting all the right spots. My legs begin to shake. Now a third finger joins the other two, pulsing inside me, and I'm ready to drop to my hands and knees and beg him to fuck me.

Slap.

I want to cry out, but the pull towards the pleasure stops me.

Slap.

I arch my back at the pleasure and pain of it.

He strokes my butt cheeks again as his fingers keep working their magic.

"You still with me, Mooi?" his voice rumbles.

My thoughts are no longer coherent as I try to remain standing.

Slap.

"Shit."

"Words," he growls, and I'll be damned if that didn't just turn me on more.

I lick my parched lips. "I'm with you." I want to beg him for my release, I want to beg him for anything and everything, but most of all, I want to beg him not to stop.

"Good." He suddenly pulls his fingers from inside me, and I whimper. I actually whimper, like a child. I can sense his face close to my own. "You smell good on my fingers." His warm breath tickles my nose, and his voice is smooth like silk. I hear him sucking, and wonder if I really taste that good.

Damn it, I want a taste too. I pucker my lips and stick my tongue out.

"Want a taste?"

I almost nod my head but then remember his 'words' rule. "Yes."

"Mmm." He teases my lips with his moist fingers. I desperately use my tongue to try and make contact, but he cleverly moves them to the opposite direction. "Then you shall have one."

I open my mouth wide in anticipation of receiving, a smile on my lips.

"Later."

"Wh-what?" My smile turns upside down, and I'm back to whimpering.

"On your knees," he orders.

"On my what?" No need to think about those words, 'cause they just came tumbling out of my mouth like a leaking faucet.

He laughs at my comment, and it sounds like he is behind me. My question is answered quickly as he helps me down. I'm shocked when I feel the pillow beneath my knees. *When did he do that?*

"I want you to use that beautiful mouth of yours and suck me."

Well shit, yeah. He just offered me my favorite meal of the day; McMagnum Deluxe, hold the onions, please.

I instinctively reach for him but my hands are tied. Instead, Magnum stands in front of me and guides his tip to my lips. I lick around the mushroom tip, the salty taste of precum on my tongue.

Mmmmm, my favorite.

I never realized how difficult this would be without the use of my hands but we make it work. He guides my head and I take him fully in my mouth till I almost gag when he hits the back of my throat.

Locking my jaw in the perfect position to receive him and his piercings, I move my head up and down his long hard shaft and realize that I now have the power. His piercings rub against my tongue in the most delightful way. If there is one thing I'm good at, it's head. If only I could use my hands to cup his balls, I would make this man sit up and beg while he calls me "Mommy."

I smile at the thought as my head bobs up and down. His grip tightens on my hair, signaling he's close. I suddenly pull away, and he lets out a loud gasp of disappointment.

171

"Words, Magnum. I need the words." I lick my tongue playfully around my lips and tilt my head up, my eyes still cloaked in darkness.

He chuckles out loud. "Touché."

I try to rise but stumble. He immediately wraps his arms around me and lifts me, carrying me God knows where. Who said sight was overrated?

"Front or back?" he murmurs.

"Back." I want the full penetration when he slams into me. Also, if I really must admit, I want him to be able to slap me from behind.

"Back it is, Mooi." He places me on the bed and unties my hands quickly.

I immediately reach for the blindfold, but he gently removes my hands.

"Not yet. The sensation will be higher when you're blindfolded."

A higher sensation? Well, sign me up for that!

"On your back. We aren't finished playing just yet."

"B-but…"

"On your back, Mooi, don't make me ask you again." His tone is stern but still playful.

I do as he asks and scoot to what feels like the middle of the bed and lay flat on my back. The sheets are cool and send chills up and down my body. I shiver involuntarily.

"Cold? I got something to warm you up."

Before I can open my mouth to give him the words, I feel a warmish liquid drop on to my stomach. It drizzles before it stops midway. What is that?

As if reading my mind, Magnum says, "Wax. How does it feel?"

I try to think focus on my sense of touch. It's not too hot, and he's right; it did warm me up. "Okay."

"Good." He plunges my three friends back inside of me. God, I missed them. Let us never part again.

I mewl and move around on the bed.

"Shhh, Mooi. Stay still." *Easy for him to say.* He slides his fingers in and out of me so achingly slow that I'm panting. And just like that, the wax is poured on my skin again as he relentlessly finger fucks me. I want to give into the burn of the wax, but I can't concentrate because of the building orgasm inside me.

I feel like I'm on one of those rollercoaster rides that's traveling closer to the sky, and you can't see the top, but you know that when you get there, it will be one hell of an exhilarating drop.

I bite my bottom lip as the buildup climbs higher and higher, and ever so higher. I can visualize myself on my tippy

173

toes reaching for this orgasm. *Oh yeah, come to me, baby. I almost have you in my reach.*

And he snatches my friends away.

No. No, no. *No.* I sit up angrily and reach out blindly. I hear the bedsheets ruffle and feel the bed dip. He quickly hoists me in the air and flips me on my stomach, slamming into me, stoking the burn inside. The burn that his fingers couldn't reach. I arch my back so tight I must look like a bow ready to let loose an arrow.

He rides me hard as he holds me up, and I match him thrust for thrust. The hairs on his thighs tickle me, heightening my senses further. Without sight, I can only feel. And I feel *everything*. Every inch of his delicious jeweled dick pounding inside me. I reach behind me till I find his hand. I try to lift it to slap me on my ass cheeks, but then I remember the words.

"I want you to fuck the shit out of me while slapping my ass."

He lets out a loud growl and does just as I request.

The old springs in the bed are squeaking too loud. *Or is that my sharper senses?*

"Harder," I scream. I'm close, so very close, and I need this so bad. I'm reaching for it, reaching, reaching...I feel his dick expand, stretching me further. One of his hands clutches my side so tight, I know there will be a bruise later, but I'll wear it like a badge of honor. The other hand still slaps my ass with each thrust, and we have lift off.

The scream that escapes my mouth starts out low and quickly builds in volume till my voice begins to crack. All thoughts of the paper-thin walls and his mother sitting downstairs scowling leave my mind. My body shakes as if it's an earthquake. We can call it Earthquake Magnum of epic proportions. Every nerve ending in my body tingles.

I'm so weak I can't hold myself up any further, but he holds me in place till I feel his dick slacken, and he lets out a guttural roar.

He places me on my back, because I'm too weak to do it myself, and collapses beside me. Somehow I find the energy to lay on his chest, our bodies slick with sweat. My eyes flicker open and closed, and I can't make up my mind if I want to pass out or enjoy this further. I give in to the sleep that overtakes me.

***

I wake with a start, surprised that I can see. Sometime after I drifted off, he must've removed my makeshift blindfold. I reach out for him, but the other side of the bed is empty and cold. I sit up to see him lounging in the chair that he brought over from his desk earlier.

"Magnum?" I stretch and feel the pulling sensation from below.

Yummy.

"I was just watching you sleep." He looks and sounds content.

I smile and pat the spot next to me. "Well, you can get an up close view if you want."

He smiles and walks over, and I scoot over to make room for him. He settles his back onto the headboard, and I nestle myself into his chest. Perfect; I fit perfectly.

"Was I too rough?" He kisses the top of my head.

I no longer feel the sting on my ass, and since I'm sitting on it, it feels fine. "No, not at all."

"Good." He exhales. "Was this something you liked?"

Is he joking? "Did I like?" I stand up on my knees and turn to face him. "Magnum, I more than liked. I *loved*."

He searches my eyes for a moment before a smile appears. "Good. We'll keep taking it slow."

"If you say so." I can't help the disappointment in my voice.

He cups my face and kisses my forehead. "I do say so."

"Magnum, I'm not fragile. I won't break."

He smiles broadly. "I know. But I still need to make sure you're adjusted to this. Do this for me."

When I look at him, his eyes are pleading and I'm still throbbing for him, yet I can't help but to give in. "Yes, I will." I give him the words that he needs.

His face relaxes. "We should get going, Mooi."

"Now?" I look towards the window; it's dark and only streetlights shine.

"Yeah, we're done here. Our journey together begins back home."

He says home, but I know he means Upstate New York, where his house, our hideaway, is. Oddly, even though I've only spent a short amount of time there, it does feel like home. Even scarier, it feels like our home.

"Yes, let's go home."

He helps me out of the bed and we shower together in the small club-footed tub. Somehow we make it work, and he even manages some vanilla sex in there. I'll never look at a shower head the same way again. Toe-curling good.

With my funeral dress on, I go into my bedroom to change clothes and pack. I jump and yelp loudly when I turn on the light to the sight of Magnum's mother sitting on my bed, waiting for me, a fight brewing in her eyes. How long has she been there?

"Mrs. Miller?" I stammer, my hand over my heart.

She looks at me, but through me. "He's always been weak. He was born a preemie, two months early." She holds up two fingers. "We didn't think he would make it. He was so small, you know." The tiniest of smiles form on her face as she relives the memory. "He weighed three pounds and six ounces."

A pang goes through my heart at the thought that I almost never met him because of this.

She rises from the bed and walks over to the window, pulling back the curtain and staring out into nothingness. "His father stayed at the hospital, morning and night, only washing up quickly in the bathroom because he was afraid to leave his son's side." She rubs the back of her neck. "His legacy." She places her hand on the window. "When the doctors finally said that CJ would live, his father rejoiced." She turns around to look at me. "Gave out cigars to just about everyone on the maternity ward. He was so proud of his little fighter. He swore on that day he would raise his son to be stronger than he ever was. No one was going to push CJ down the way the world did him."

My blood boils at that last part, and my fists clench together. "What about his own father pushing him down?" I quip.

Her eyebrows crinkle in confusion. "Oh no, he was just making a man out of him. That's why he was so tough."

This woman is batshit crazy. "What about the scars?"

She closes her eyes and shakes her head. "Scars heal."

Does she not know the reason behind the tattoos?

"Oh yeah, they may heal, but they do leave a mark." I refuse to tell her about Magnum's night terrors. She doesn't deserve that information.

"Everything his father did was out of love. But CJ was just so weak."

"No, your husband was the weak one. Don't put your husband's mental illness on Mag."

178

Her eyes widen in shock. "He wasn't ill. He was just tough, that's all."

"He beat your son senseless, and you stood by and watched." My voice is accusatory, and I don't give a shit.

"He was making him stronger," she repeats, wringing her hands together.

That's when it dawns on me. She needs to believe this or else that means she's failed as well.

"Why didn't you help your son when he needed you?"

She turns away and faces the wall. "There was nothing I could do to help."

I take a step towards her. "Like hell there wasn't. You could've packed your stuff and taken him away from this madness." I spread my arms out. "Instead, you lost him for not being there."

She spins around to face me again. "I was there." Her voice shakes.

"No. No, you weren't." I throw my hands up in exasperation, giving up. She needs to find her own path, and she's not my concern; Magnum is. I begin the process of gathering my things to leave, in silence. She watches my every move. I grab my cellphone from the nightstand, and walk towards the door, my hand on the light switch. "Until you come to terms with the truth, I suggest you not contact him."

I turn the lights out and close the door behind me, shocked to see Magnum standing there.

His eyes betray nothing, but I know.

"You heard?"

He looks at the door before looking back at me. He reaches and takes my bag. "Come on. Let's go home, Mooi."

I follow him down the stairs and out of his childhood home, leaving the past behind us. He helps me into the passenger seat, and I buckle up as he places our bags in the trunk. Once he's in the driver's seat, I finally feel relaxed. He takes my hand in his as he pulls off. With my free hand, I pull out my cell to check my emails. No voicemail messages yet, since no one has my new number.

Some of my co-workers emailed to check in on me. I smile at some of their funny messages and shoot off quick replies as he drives. Ray also sent me an email, begging me to contact him as soon as possible. But an email catches me by surprise. swalsh@tmail.com. *Stew?* I click on it to open.

Dear Brenda,

I've been trying to reach you for a few days. I even went by your house, but no one was home. I have an update on what I've found. Please call me as soon as you get this.

Best,

Stew

I look over at Magnum as he concentrates on driving. He looks so cute.

"I got an email from Stew."

He turns to look at me briefly. "What did he say?"

"He has an update for me."

"That's it?"

I shrug. "Well, yeah. He said to call him as soon as I get this message."

He glances over at me again. "Well, give him a call."

I look at the time on my phone; it shows that it's ten at night. Stew is up, either working or not, so I dial. It rings a few times before someone answers.

"Hello?" a woman's voice speaks.

I look at my phone to make sure I dialed the right number.

"Umm, this is Brenda. I'm looking for Stew. Stewart Walsh."

"Brenda? He's told me so much about you." Her voice cracks.

Something is off, and my heart sinks to the pit of my stomach.

"You must be his wife, Christine." I smile into the phone, pushing down the dread that has settled around me.

"Yes, and I want to thank you for calling during this time. Thank you for thinking of our family."

I reach out and grab for Magnum's hand again. He takes it and squeezes it, giving me his reassurance that all will be okay. "Umm, Christine." I'm breathing heavily on the phone, trying not to cry. "Did something happen?"

"Oh." There's a long pause before she proceeds, "I thought you knew." She exhales, and I can hear her choked back tears. "Stew died of a heart attack at work."

She's still talking but I drop the phone, and it falls to my lap. Magnum pulls over to the side of the highway, grabbing my phone and placing it to his ear. I'm too stunned to look at him as he listens intently to what Christine is saying. He nods into the speaker as if she could see him.

Eventually, he hangs up without saying a word.

"Stew." I cry out, placing my hands over my face. I sob heavily. He looked so healthy when we saw him a few weeks ago.

"I'll get us home now."

Chapter 22

Renegades ~ X-Ambassadors

Magnum

I spend the next couple of days comforting Brenda over the loss of her friend. She blames herself for adding to his stress and causing his heart attack. Now that Stew is dead, I need to pick up where he left off with his research. I called his wife the day after our initial phone call and asked her if she had any of his case notes from Brenda. She said she did and was helpful in scanning and emailing them to us.

Based on Stew's notes, he went to the prison where Brenda's ex was locked up and eventually died. Or I guess you could say killed; he was shanked in a prison riot. Her ex's old cellmate was released a few years back, and Stew was on the verge of tracking him down to speak to him. But he died before he was able to. A shocker did come out of the notes. Turns out Dr. Raymond Cross did part of his premed at the prison. I knew there was a reason why I didn't like that asshole. There was a notation that he was going to speak to the good ol' doc the day he died. So, now I have plans to speak to him in the near future and when I say near future, I mean today. Difference is, he won't see me coming.

"Mag, I really don't think Ray could do anything like this," Brenda pleads with me as we get dressed.

"Mooi, I'm not accusing him of anything." Not. "I just want to ask him a few questions."

She looks at me apprehensively before nodding. "Just promise me that you won't hit him or anything."

I smile wickedly at her, crossing my fingers behind me while sauntering over to her slowly. "I promise. He will get the benefit of the doubt. Just have a few questions." I pull her in to me for a kiss, squeezing her to me. "Mooi, I love you, and there isn't anything I won't do to protect you."

"I know," she says breathlessly. "I love you too, but Ray is a good friend and I trust him."

My gut is telling me that there is more to Dr. Raymond Cross but instead, I reply, "I know, baby. Let's go before it gets too late."

Because driving to the city would take too long, I charter a flight for us, what would normally be a five-hour commute is cut down to just an hour and a half.

I pull up in the rental car to the doctor's recently purchased condo, which is conveniently five blocks from Brenda's house. He is looking more and more suspect to me but I don't let my reservations come out.

"Mooi, I think you should wait in the car for me."

She spins her head to face me, and her perfume wafts throughout the small area. "Absolutely not."

"Didn't think you would," I grumble as I open the door.

Hand and hand, we talk to the building. Once inside the elevator, I lay down some quick ground rules that I know she will most likely ignore.

"Let me do the talking and stay near me at all times."

She tosses her auburn hair to the back. "He will talk more freely with me. I should do the talking."

"Mooi…" I say as the elevator door opens. We stare at each other for a moment before she sashays that cute ass of hers off the elevator. By time I catch up to her, she is already ringing the doorbell.

The door swings open and the doc stands with his wallet in his hand and his cellphone to his ear. It takes him a moment to register that we must not be his food delivery.

"Ugh, let me call you back," he murmurs into the phone. "Bren?"

The familiarity of the way he says her name makes me instantly jealous. She told me how they almost dated and for that alone, I don't trust him around her.

"Hi Ray. Sorry to disturb you." She turns to look at me standing behind her. Good ol' doc looks at me with apprehension.

"Magnum?" A crease forms on his forehead. "Umm, sorry…" He opens the door wider and gestures for us to come in. "Please, come inside."

Possessively, I take her hand in my own and I lead the way inside. The doc's eyes rest on our linked fingers. I push back the urge to tongue her down in front of him.

Locking the door behind him, he walks deeper into the open living room and takes a seat in an oversized chair. We sit on the couch, facing him.

Crossing his legs and settling into his position, he asks, "Okay, what can I do for you?"

Brenda places her hand on my knee and clears her throat. "Ray, there is someone that's trying to kill me."

He sits up in shock and leans in. "What?"

"Yes, we think whoever this person is knew my ex."

"Your ex has something to do with this?"

She shakes her head. "No, well not exactly. You see, my ex is dead. He died in a prison riot years five years ago."

"I don't think I'm following you."

Tired of the pussyfooting around, I take over. "You interned at the Adirondack Correctional Facility."

He closes his eyes briefly before nodding. "Where your ex was a prisoner." He sits back. "But I don't understand. What does this have to do with me?"

"Whoever is doing this to her is copying the exact same things that her ex did. This person had to have both known her ex *and* the details of what he did to her." I point to him. "You, doc, fit the bill."

His mouth opens in shock. "I was just an intern there. Do you know how many prisoners I saw?" He stands and begins pacing back and forth. "Trust me, I saw too many to remember any person by name. I, not once, had a personal conversation with the men I treated at that facility."

I rise as well. "But you have to admit that it's a bit strange...or shall we call it coincidental."

He faces Brenda. "Bren, you can't possibly believe that I had anything to do with what is going on with you."

She bites her bottom lip. "No, I don't but we needed to cover all bases."

Relief settles over his face. "Thank God for that."

But I'm not done with him. "Did you have an appointment with Detective Stewart Walsh last week?"

He nods slowly. "Yes, he called me and asked if he could see me. We set up a time, but he never showed up."

"Yeah, hard for him to show up when he's dead."

"Dead?" He stumbles into his chair as he tries to take a seat.

"Yeah, dead."

"B-but how?"

"Heart attack," I reply as I stare at him intently. Did he have anything to do with harassing Brenda and trying to kill her?

"Oh."

"Ray, did Stew say anything to you over the phone?"

He shakes his head. "Nothing. Just that he needed to question me, but he wouldn't say why over the phone."

I open my mouth to speak but he interrupts. "Bren, I'm sorry that I can't be of more help to you. But you have to understand that I will have to cut this questioning short. Unless you take this to the cops, I am under no obligation to answer anything further. I can't have these type of rumors circling around me."

"Then help us catch the bastard who's doing this to her," I growl.

He rises and walks to the door and opens it. "I'm sorry. There is nothing more for us to talk about."

With my fists balled, I get ready to storm over to him and force him to talk, but Brenda grabs my arm and pleads with me with her eyes. With clenched teeth, I nod my agreement and follow her to the door, but not without me giving the asshole one last glare before we leave.

Back inside the car, we sit wordlessly. I watch a delivery person go into the building, carrying bags of takeout.

"He's hiding something, Mooi."

"No. I don't believe that."

"He all but lawyered up."

"He was right. We had no business questioning him without the police." She leans her head on the window.

"But…"

"Mag, I'm tired. Just take me home. Please."

Without another word, I start the car and drive towards the airport, silently making a vow to catch this person who is after the woman I love.

Chapter 23
All of the Lights ~ Kanye West

Magnum

We arrived back at my cabin last night. Brenda barely said a word on the flight, and even less when we arrived home. This woman that I love, who has always been a fighter, suddenly seems defeated and I don't know how to make this shit better for her, other than catch the fucker. She literally felt like she was drifting away from me and the only way I knew to anchor us both was to make love to her until she collapsed in my arms and drifted off to sleep.

This morning, I decide to speak to the cellmate, Anthony Fordham. With some quick digging, I found an old address prior to his imprisonment. I couldn't find anything current but at least it's a start. He apparently lived in a city not too far from here called Utica. I reach out to Manny to help me in my search.

Manny kicks back on my couch and opens a fresh pack of Newports so he can feed his nicotine addiction.

I shake my head. "I told you, no smoking inside the house. Take that shit outside." I point to the door.

With his unlit cigarette dangling from the side of his mouth, he huffs, "Man, really? You made me take a seven-hour drive to bumfuck nowhere, and I can't smoke in your house?" He points at me with his index and pointer finger, the cigarette resting in between the two.

Seven hours? I forgot Grandma Moses sitting in front of me drives slower than molasses dripping in the dead of winter.

"Outside," I reiterate.

He grumbles and takes his cancer sticks with him.

"Close the door behind you." I laugh loudly as he slams the door, causing Brenda to come out of our bedroom to see what's going on.

"Mag?" She tightens her bathrobe around her and she pitter patters on bare feet. "Everything okay?"

It's one in the afternoon, and she's in her robe. Its uncharacteristic of her, but I won't press.

I stand and walk over to her, the need to have her in my arms strong. "Manny got upset that I made him go outside to smoke, that's all."

Relief, and then confusion settles on her face. "Manny? What time is it?"

"One." I kiss the top of her head and lead her to the couch, where she sits on my knee and leans her head on my shoulder.

"I slept that long?" She yawns.

I squeeze her tight to me, never wanting to let her go. "Mmmhmm." We did some rather exhausting activities last night before we went to sleep, or I should say, before we passed out but still...she did sleep much longer than usual.

"I should get dressed."

My mind drifts to getting her naked again; under me, on top of me, in front of me. There are so many positions I want to do to her, try with her.

I place my hand on her belt and tug at it friskily, while playfully trailing kisses down her neck. She moans, her head rolling back.

"You better not start what you can't finish."

"Oh, I can finish. Trust and believe I can finish." Even if I gotta lock that damn front door, leaving Manny out there banging to get in.

Mmmm, that does sound like a doable idea.

"What about Manny?" Her hand is on my cheek as I kiss my way down to her chest.

"Manny who?" I murmur against her warm skin. I part her legs so I can slide my fingers inside her.

She closes her legs tight, trapping my exploring hand. "What is Manny doing here?"

I groan and stop trying to make her have an orgasm on my lap. "I reached out to him last night. I'm going to follow the lead on your ex's cellmate."

Her eyes brighten. "Do you think this will lead to anything?"

I shrug. "I sure hope it does."

She rises and gives me a quick kiss. "Then I guess we should get going. I'm going to change clothes."

I raise an eyebrow at her. "We? No, Mooi. Manny and I are going. I need you here, protected and safe."

"But Magnum, I think I should go with you. Why would I expect you and Manny to do all of my dirty work?"

She's so cute when she's like this. "Because I'm your man and you will allow me to help you, the way you helped me."

"That was different."

I shake my head. "Nothing different about it." I take her hands in mine. "Let me do this for you. It's what I do best." We've never had the discussion about exactly what I do for Tony, but since Cyma is her best friend, I'm sure she has an inkling of it. Never in my life did I think that what I do for him would be beneficial in helping the woman I love. If I've ever felt guilty in the past for the blood on my hands, I no longer do. I'm now thankful for it, and I would do it all over again if I can save her.

She places her plump lips on mine. I devour her, wishing only we could blend into one.

"Ahhhem." We both turn to see Manny, with Cyma and Anaya behind him.

Straightening her robe with a nice rosy blush on her cheeks, Brenda turns to look at her friends. "Mag didn't say you were coming over." She walks over to hug them.

"Well, he called last night and gave us the details. Told us we needed to spend some time with you today." Cyma hugs her friend tight to her, tears in her eyes. "I can't believe you didn't call and tell me what was going on."

Brenda wipes at her own tears. "You just had the baby, and I didn't want to put this on you."

"You're more than a friend to me; you're my sister. I want you to always feel free to talk to me. I'm never too busy for you."

"Same here. I can't believe you didn't call me either. I didn't recently have a baby. I would've helped in any way I could." Anaya joins in, making it a group hug.

"Can I get a hug too?" Manny teases from behind them. Eyerolls and air kisses are thrown his way.

I rise and walk over. "Mooi, Manny and I need to get going. Let me speak to you in the back for a sec."

"Ladies, go ahead and settle in. The bar and fridge are stocked." Brenda waves at the group as I take her hand and lead her to the back.

"Shit, that was better than Mag offered me when I first arrived. The most he said to me was to go outside to smoke."

Once in the bedroom, I shut the door behind us.

"Promise me you won't leave the house."

She rolls her eyes and looks back to me. "Mag, I'm fine. No one knows I'm out here."

I hold her face in the palms of my hand. "Mooi, promise me."

She places her hands on my wrists. "Alright, I promise."

I kiss her quickly. It's quick enough to not begin ripping her clothes off but long enough to let her know I'll miss her. This will be the first time we'll be away from each other in several weeks. Shit, I didn't realize how hard this would be.

"Thank you. I should go." I'm already having second thoughts about leaving her alone, with only her friends as protection. I'll never forgive myself if something happens to her. I look longingly at the bed that seems so empty without the two of us in it.

She opens the door, and we walk down the hall, arm and arm.

Cyma gives us the thumbs up, and Anaya nods her approval. Manny, on the other hand, is searching for his pack of cigarettes.

"Thank you, Cyma, Anaya, for coming out on short notice."

Cyma waves me off. "No need to thank us, just go and get the bastard that's doing this to her."

One last kiss, and Manny and I are out the door and in my car.

"So how far is this Utica place from here?" Manny tries to light his cigarette, but I snatch the lighter and throw it out the window. "Hey!"

"No smoking in the car. It's far enough." If he keeps it up, I will snatch those cigarettes and toss them too.

He huffs and scrunches down in his seat. "Wake me when we're there." He folds his arms over his chest and closes his eyes.

Utica, here we come. Hope you're ready for us because I'm bringing hell with me.

Chapter 24
Love the Way You Lie ~ Eminem feat. Rihanna

Brenda

I blend up another batch of milkshakes. Since Cyma is nursing, Anaya and I both agree not to drink without her. What are besties for? Apparently, not getting drunk together these days, that's for sure.

I hand each of them a glass and take a sip from mine, wishing it had some rum in it.

Crossing her legs and sitting back on the couch, Anaya begins, "So, tell us what's up with you and Mag?"

Folding her legs underneath her, Cyma chimes in, "You two look absolutely cute together." She takes another sip of her milkshake. "Oh my goodness, I really shouldn't be drinking this with all the baby weight I've gained."

Anaya and I both look at her, and I'm the first to object. "Are you kidding? If we could all look the way you do right now, puh-leeze , I would get knocked up in a New York minute."

Anaya raises her glass in agreement. "Here, here."

Cyma rolls her eyes. "Let's get back to the dirt on you and Mag."

Anaya's eyes light up. "Yes, let's." She leans in, waiting for me to begin.

I'm not ashamed of what we do, but I don't know if I want to talk about it with them. It just seems too intimate, and I don't think words could ever do it justice. I don't believe they would judge me, but I don't think they would understand it either.

I cross my legs, one over the other, and swing the top one up and down. "Oh, nothing to share, really."

They both look disappointed.

"At least tell me the sex is mind-blowing," Cyma urges.

My mouth drops open because it's not like her to want to talk about sex so openly. "Ummm..."

"I haven't had sex in months. Months, you hear me? "She clasps her hands in front of her. "I'm begging you. Please share whatever you can. I live vicariously through the two of you right now."

Anaya and I both laugh at her remarks as she pouts.

Well, I'm not the person to let my best friend down, so I decide to at least give her something. "Yes, the sex is mind-blowing." In ways, they would never understand.

Cyma looks at me like a puppy waiting for its master to feed it.

"Umm, well he has introduced me to some things in sex that I realize I like." There, that is as far as it will go with me dishing.

Now they are both on the edge of their seat.

Perhaps I've chosen my words wrong. "I, uh, I mean..."

Anaya beckons me to proceed with her hand. "And?"

"Let's just say, we're made for each other." I refuse to tell them about the piercings on his dick; that's personal, and I consider it mine.

They both sit back in the seat, either bored with me or annoyed. I'm thinking a little of both. So I decide to switch the subject. "How is my goddaughter, Hope? Any new pics of her?"

Cyma's face brightens as she fishes through her purse for her cell. She clicks on it a few times and hands it to me. I stare at Hope and her older sister Lelia, and there are some with Anaya's son, Xavier, smiling. This almost makes me want kids, a thought that has never really crossed my mind before. I flip through all the pictures, each one cuter than the last.

"Any more?" I hand her the phone back.

"Oh, I posted more on my social media account."

I haven't been online in weeks, so I grab my laptop from the kitchen island and power it up. Quickly, I log onto my account and click on her profile to look at some more pictures. I ooh and ahh over each and every one of them. Kids can grow up so fast. I can't wait to get her to my hou-. Reality hits me; my house is in Queens. Magnum said this is our house, our hideaway. Would that make my house in Queens ours as well? Are we taking things to that level where he would move in with me? How come he and I never had this talk before?

Deep down inside, I know I want him with me, day and night. I'm missing him terribly now and it's only been a few hours.

"Bren. Something wrong?" Anaya asks with a look of concern.

I wave her off. "Oh no. Not at all." I click back to my newsfeed to see what else I've missed. Pictures from a co-workers' honeymoon, I click 'love'. Pictures from Anaya's latest design project, 'love'. I like, love, or show the angry face at a few postings till I get to a post of a picture of Finster.

David posted it a few days ago. The caption reads "feeling heartbroken." There are a bunch of sad faces underneath the picture of Fin. What the hell happened? I see he's online, so I initiate a chat with him.

Me: What happened to Fin?

David: He was struck by a car. Bastard hit him and kept going.

Me: (crying face emoji as well as in real life) Oh no. That is horrible.

David: The vet said he was killed instantly, so I guess I should take comfort in the fact that he didn't suffer.

Me: Oh, David. I wish there were something I could do for you.

David: (heart emoji)

Another message block opens up on my computer. It's from my co-worker, Kim.

Kim: Did you hear?

Me: Hear what?

Kim: Dr. Cross was arrested last night. He wrote scrips for a potentially lethal cocktail.

My heart sinks as the room begins to spin. I try desperately to focus as nausea hits me.

Me: What?

Kim: The hospital did their typical inventory check on supplies and saw they were missing Potassium Chloride and Pancuronium Bromide.

Those two medications can induce a heart attack. Oh my God...he couldn't...he wouldn't... Oh, my God. I reach for my cell and call Magnum, but it goes to voicemail so I leave him a message to call me right away.

David: Bren? Are you there?

I forgot all about him during my messaging with Kim. I go back to him immediately to offer whatever comfort I can.

Chapter 25
Maria Maria ~ Carlos Santana feat. The Product G & B

Magnum

The GPS leads us to a small rundown house on Dwyer Avenue. We both get out of the car and look up and down the sleepy street. No one is out, not even walking a dog. Most of the houses look like they're long overdue for a paint job.

"Where the fuck are we?" asks Manny, who dressed down for the occasion in a Polo tee, jeans, and Timbs, unlike his usual city attire, which consists of a Tom Ford suit.

"Welcome to Utica," I joke. Seriously, this street reminds me of the one from Halloween but with raggedy houses. I'm half-expecting Michael Myers to pop out. I place my hand on my holster to make sure my gun is there, just in case.

"Alright, let's get this shit over with." Manny points his head in the direction of the house we're looking for.

We climb the steps and knock on the door, and wait. And wait. And wait some more.

"I haven't seen anyone live in that house in years."

We both turn around to see an older man with a long white beard. Not like Santa; a little dingier than that. When I say a little, I mean I can see exactly what this man has eaten over the course of a few hours all through his beard. I guess he's saving some for later.

"Oh yeah? Do you know where they might've moved to?" Manny asks, walking down the steps with me following behind.

"Not really sure. I think I heard they moved downstate." He strokes his beard as flecks of old scrambled eggs come off.

"No, they stayed in the area." Another voice sounds from behind the man. An older woman appears, bent over with her cane. It must be at least seventy degrees out, and she has on a down coat.

Manny smiles and bows to her. "Why thank you, ma'am. Do you know whereabouts they went?"

Since when does he speak Upstate talk?

She strokes her chin which has a beard that is second runner-up to the old man. Not as long but just as thick. "Hmm, let me see. After Anthony got arrested, that gal of his moved somewhere around here."

Bingo. "What was he arrested for?" I pry.

Her eyes narrow through her glasses. She shakes her head. "Couldn't say." She looks down the street.

Manny and I both look at each other, and he gives me a wink.

"So, tell me the two of you are married?" Manny, who was born and raised in the Bronx, lays on a thick Puerto Rican accent that he really doesn't have.

The older man shakes his head. "Oh no, we're neighbors."

"So, you mean this pretty young thing isn't taken?" Manny walks over and helps the older woman cross the street. She happily places her arm through his.

Yeah, we'll have the dirt in no time at all, with Mister Smooth over there.

I stand with the older man, and he stares at my piercings and tats.

"I used to be in the Navy." He tries to unbutton his shirt sleeve to, I assume, roll it up and show me his body art. He gets frustrated and stops. "Damn arthritis."

"What's your stamp?" I ask.

"Nothing as elaborate as yours." He points to my tribal art on my scalp. "Mine has a heart with my dead wife's name on it."

"My condolences."

He waves his hand at me. "No need. She was a bitch. Divorced her soon as I got out. Been with a pretty little gal ever since. Best decision of my life." He laughs out loud, and I laugh with him. After a while, he stops and looks at me. "What you coming around here asking about Anthony for?"

Well, that was straight to the point. He's growing on me. "Need to ask him some questions about a cellmate of his."

He nods. "I see. Well, I don't know where he went when he came out." He does the 'crazy' sign. "That boy was loco, if you know what I mean. He was into everything from tipping cows, to blowing up a neighbor's car, to beating up his girl."

I listen intently; any information on who he is useful.

"His mom and dad did everything they could to help him. When he was arrested, they moved out of this town for good. But his girlfriend stayed for a bit." He turns and points to the house. "But she left when he came out. Not sure where they went."

"Well, thank you, sir. The information you gave was extremely helpful."

He starts walking down the street. "Well, not sure if I was of any help but that was all the information I know. Good luck with your search."

Manny runs across the street just as the old man walks away. "Alright, let's roll."

"Roll where?" My brows furrow.

He holds up his cell. "I got an address."

I start walking towards the car. "Shit, hurry up and let's go."

We drive outside of town, deeper into the country. There are mostly farm pastures in this area. The GPS leads us to a general area, but we have to figure out the exact location of the house. After a while, we find it and drive up to the rundown farm house. I see someone staring at us from the window, but I can't make out who the person is. As we get out of the car and walk to the door, the person opens it immediately, staring at us with her hands crossed over her chest.

Manny speaks first. "Excuse me, Miss. Are you Marie?"

Chapter 26

Magnum

Manny and I accept the cans of soda Marie offers us, as we sit amongst the animal kingdom in her house. She must have at least twenty cats, ten dogs, and some other animals roaming around. She picks one of the cats up from the chair before she sits and places the jet-black adult cat on her lap, stroking it with one hand while sipping from her can of Cola from the other.

"I really don't know what I can tell you that you already don't know about Anthony." Another cat nuzzles at her ankles, begging for attention.

Thank God Manny and I don't suffer from allergies, or this would be hell.

"Well, anything you can tell us would be great."

"I haven't seen him or heard from him in years."

"Why was he arrested?" Stew's file didn't have certain details in it; guess it wasn't necessary since it wasn't an official investigation.

"Oh that, he got carried away one night. He wouldn't let me leave the house and beat the shit out of me. I ran for my life in the middle of the night." She says this so casually, as if she was asking us to pass her the salt.

Manny and I exchange glances. "So you went back to him after he got out?" Manny asks.

She nods. "That's the reason why he got out on parole. He sent me letters through his lawyer, begging my forgiveness and that he did it because he loved me. So I decided to forgive him and speak at his parole hearing, telling them that I believed he was a changed man."

A man beat and kidnapped her, and she forgave him?

"When he got out on parole, he had to have an address to come home to. Where did he go?" I press.

"We stayed at his parents' old house in Utica. Everything was great between us in the beginning. He got a job and was going to therapy for all his issues. He kept his regular parole appointments and drug and alcohol testings." Her voice strains at the last sentence.

I wait a beat before pushing for more answers. "Did he fall off the wagon or something?"

She shakes her head, her eyes watering. "No. He didn't have those types of issues. That's just mandatory of parolees. It was after his parole was up; that's when he changed. It was like something in him snapped." She bends, placing the soda on the floor, and picks up the other cat.

"He went back to his old self?" Manny pries.

"No. It was worse. Much, much worse. It was like something in him was dead. He had no empathy, like he hated the world."

"Where did he go?" I sit on the edge of the couch. I'm tired of pussyfooting around with this.

She looks away. "I don't know. He went to work, and I packed up and left. It was hard to do in a small town like Utica. But I managed it." She looks me straight in the eye as she tells this.

"Any suggestions of where you think he might be?" Manny sets his soda on the coffee table.

"No." She rises, and both cats jump off her lap and scurry off.

Manny and I both stand and walk towards the door when my eye settles on a painting on her wall. It isn't the best-looking abstract art I've seen, but there is something about it that seems so familiar.

"Mag?" Manny calls out from the door, but I'm too transfixed on the painting.

She walks up behind me. "He painted that. He took up art when he was in prison. Said it was the only thing that calmed the voices in his head." She taps her pointer finger to her temple.

I stare at the signature of the painting. "But that signature doesn't say Anthony."

She smiles and shakes her head. "Oh no. He decided to start going by his dead kid brother's name. David."

The blood drains from my face as my heart pounds thunderously in my chest.

Chapter 27

Brenda

I arrive at Forestport where David asked me to meet him. This is the place he and Finster used to spend long weekends. He wants to spread Fin's ashes near the trail where they would take long walks. I had a hard time convincing Cyma and Anaya to allow me to go because of the madman who is after me, but I promise them that David is harmless. Cyma, having met David a few times, decided it was okay for me to skip out of the house for a few hours. I promised them that I would keep checking in. But I just had to be there for David. He and Fin were so close, and I loved Fin as well.

I walk through the path of brush towards the house David rented out. The tiny house finally comes into view, and David is outside painting.

"David." I wave to him, and he turns and runs towards me.

"You made it." He hugs me excitedly.

"Of course I would. I promised you, didn't I?"

He loops his arm through mine and leads me to his painting.

"What do you think?" he asks.

I stare at the weird abstract painting and try to figure out what all the forms and shapes are.

"It's great," I lie. It's just as bad as the one he gave me last year that hangs in my hallway. Never did figure out that one either.

"Good, it's yours," he beams.

My heart drops. What am I going to do with *two* bad paintings? But I don't have the heart to say no since he's hurting over the loss of Finster. "Wonderful." My smile is tight as I try to be polite.

"Say nothing of it. I just wanted to show my appreciation of you. Today is such a special day."

I guess spreading his dog's ashes constitutes as a special day for him. Who am I to judge. "Yes, yes, it is. I'm just happy to be here for you."

"This wouldn't be possible without you, Brenda." He holds my shoulders, and a cold shiver goes up my spine. I want to shrug him off, but politeness prevails.

I look around. "Umm, should we get started? I have to get back to the house before Mag gets home. He's going to be pissed with me as it is."

His eyes narrow. "He doesn't know where you are?"

"Oh no. I snuck out without telling him. He hasn't a clue." I smile.

"Good. I don't think I liked him." He turns and heads towards the house, but there is something in his voice that gives me pause. Something seems off, and I don't know what it is.

He turns around and stares at me, a warm smile on his face. "Coming?"

I shake those doubts out of my head. I'm sure I'm just paranoid because of my own personal drama. Why am I transmitting it to poor David? "Of course." I smile and jog up the steps.

The house is minimalist at best. There is a couch, a stove, a fridge, a sink, and a bathroom. That's about it. I look around the surroundings, which literally takes only a second, and I wonder how he possibly comes here so often.

"I don't have much to offer. I got some bottled water and some pop."

"I'll just take a water," I say as I stare out of the window.

Not seconds later, he hands me a bottle over my shoulder, causing me to jump.

"Oh, you scared me." I take the bottle and open it, taking a large swig.

"Sorry about that." He walks over to the couch and takes a seat, patting the empty space next to him.

I hesitate to get comfortable because I really need to get back before Mag gets home. Perhaps I should call him.

"Come on, I promise we'll go shortly. Just sit and talk with me about Fin for a while."

I push my apprehension aside and sit next to him.

"He was such a loyal furry best friend."

"He was," I readily agree, taking another pull on my water.

"I just can't believe he's gone."

I place my hand on his shoulder. "Neither can I. Did you report it to the police?"

"I did." He nods.

I smile at him but then I start to feel slightly dizzy. I shake my head to get my orientation, but it's not working. *What's going on?*

"Brenda, are you okay?"

"I-I don't know." I try to stand but collapse on the couch, my head hitting the back.

"Dizzy?"

"Yaasss." My speech is now slurring. *What's happening to me?* I go through the list of medical possibilities in my head. Stroke? Possibly. I try desperately to come to a medical conclusion.

"Don't worry, just give into it. It's not painful. It will just knock you out for a few hours while I take care of some things."

Again, I try to stand, but it feels like waves knocking me over as I fall back down.

"As I was saying. I did report it to the police. Your cop friend...Stew, I think was his name, was very helpful. I even met him at his station with some coffee and donuts."

I try to focus on what he's saying, but I'm drifting away.

He strokes my hair, the same way I've seen him do with Fin. "Shame that he was digging a little too deep for comfort, so I took care of him. It was rather easy. When I saw Dr. Cross come to visit you that day, that's when the beginning of a plan took place. Never knew how easy it would be. I went to the hospital and pretended to run into him. So easy to snatch his keys to his office." He bends down closer to my face. "But the brilliant part of my plan was when I was able to steal his fingerprints and hack into the database to write the prescription that killed your cop friend. I'll tell you, the things you can find on YouTube is amazing. I sprinkled the cocktail solution on the donuts. He never tasted or suspected a thing."

And that's when darkness pulls me under its waves, sweeping me away.

Chapter 28
Can't Let You Go ~ Fabolous feat. Mike Shorey & Lil' Mo

Magnum

Marie is still talking as I pull out my cellphone to call Mooi. The phone goes to voicemail. *God damn it, Brenda, pick up your phone.* I dial again, and it goes to voicemail. "You have reached Brenda Johnson. Sorry that I missed your call, but if you leave your name and your number, I will get back to you. Bye."

I decided to leave a message. "Damn it, Mooi. Call me back as soon as you get this message." I start to hang up but another thought hits me. I place the phone back to my ear. "I love you." With that, I end the call.

Marie smiles. "Your lady?"

"My everything," I correct.

Manny stands next to me. "What's up?"

I ignore him because I'm busy dialing again. The phone rings, and this time there is an answer. "Hey, Mag," Cyma's sing-song voice comes on the line.

"Where's Mooi?" I jump right the fuck over the niceties and right into business.

"Mooi?"

"Brenda," I say, annoyed that she is not in my head understanding my code language.

"Oh, so you have nicknames for each other." She laughs over the phone, clearly not understanding that I'm in *fucking nuclear* mode.

"Where is she? She's not answering her phone."

There's a long pause and I can tell she is having a muffled conversation. "Oh. Umm..."

"Spit it out." I know I'll catch hell from Tick from speaking to his wife like this, but I'll deal with him later.

Another fucking muffled conversation. "She, uh, she left a few hours ago."

"Left? Left for where?" I'm all but running out the door with my keys in my hand, Manny running behind me.

"David's dog, Finster, died. He was such a cute dog. I remember when he first brought Fin home." She goes into a whole diatribe that I don't give two shits about.

"Where did she go?"

"Oh, uh...Anaya, what was that area called again? Oh yes, it's the Forestport. It's near the Kayuta campgrounds. She left an address on the table. Wait a sec, I'll get it." This has to be the longest second of my life. She finally comes back and prattles off the address to me. I plug it into my GPS and hang up without another word.

"Call Tick and Tony. Tell them we may need back-up, and this is not a drill. This is a fucking *mission*." I peel out from Marie's dirt road and head out to the battle.

Chapter 29

Could Have Been You ~ Joss Stone

Brenda

I wake up, tied and gagged, and not in a good way, on David's couch. I open my eyes to a pounding headache, confusion, and sloppy licks on my face. Finster is lapping at my face. *Fin is alive? What happened to me?* Slowly, memories come back of David's words to me before I passed out. I try to use my tongue to push out the scarf that is tied around my mouth.

"Oh, I see you're finally awake," David says, as Finster runs around his legs.

I want to answer, but the gag is preventing me from doing that.

David cups his ear. "What's that, you say?"

I glare at him angrily and try desperately to break free of my restraints.

"Sorry, you'll have to speak up." He laughs as Fin barks loudly and runs back to lick my face some more.

At least I have one friend.

"As you can see, Fin has had a remarkable recovery." He stares at the two of us before adding, "You're still his favorite, apparently."

I guess this dog can sense an asshole quicker than I can. Story of my life. I try to move my hands that are tied behind my back, but I only cut into skin. So I look up at him and plead with my eyes. His smile shows he is enjoying this. I am supposed to check in with Cyma and Anaya every hour, and it's been several, so they must've alerted Magnum and Manny by now. If I can stay alive long enough, I might have a chance to survive.

He walks over and kneels in front of me. "If I take off the gag, you promise not to scream?"

I nod my head.

"Well, it doesn't really matter, since no one is near us anyway." He removes the gag in one swoop.

I move my jaw around, trying to get the circulation back. "Why?" I manage to say.

"Why not?" He heads to the fridge and pulls out two bottles of water. He holds one out to me and I refuse, looking away. Is he seriously trying to offer me some water after he drugged me with the other bottle a few hours ago?

Wait? How long have I been here? I'm assuming it's only hours, but what if it's been days or even worse, weeks or months. "How long have I been out?"

He walks towards me with my bottle in hand. "Two hours or so. It gave me enough time to prepare."

Prepare for what?

Again, he is taunting me with the bottle of water, shaking it in front of my face. As thirsty I am, from whatever drug he gave me, I'm not quite that thirsty.

"This one is just water." He crosses his heart. "I swear."

"No, thank you," I say through gritted teeth.

He shrugs and places it on the floor in front of the couch. "Suit yourself."

"Why me? I thought we were friends?" I can't believe I trusted him all this time.

"I thought we would be more than just friends."

I swallow hard. "It just wasn't meant to be."

"But you're with him, aren't you?"

Fear is tightening around my esophagus. I don't know the right answer. But somehow I feel that if I lie, it will be worse for me. "Yes, I am."

He sneers at me. "Figures. You dated Curtis, a brute, and now you're bumping uglies with another brute."

Curtis? How does he know my ex's name? "H-how do you know Curtis?"

He sits cross-legged on the floor and plays with Fin. "We were cellmates."

My eyes widen, and I wish I could sit up to stop the room from suddenly spinning. "Cellmates?"

"Yep, you know how he died?"

I know the story that was told to me, but the words fly out of my head, and I shake my head.

"I killed him. You ever felt the life drain from someone's body?" He doesn't wait for me to respond. Instead, he closes his eyes and leans his head back. "It's the most exhilarating thing I've ever felt."

My entire body is shaking, and my teeth begin to chatter with fear.

Slowly, he rights his head and stares at me with the emptiest eyes I've ever seen. "He talked about you a lot, you know. It wasn't till he showed me your picture that I knew you and I belonged together." He strokes Fin's thick fur on his stomach.

Nauseous; I'm feeling extremely nauseous. "I-I don't feel so well." My saliva tastes metallic and salty, which is not helping my queasy stomach.

His eyes narrow. "I offered you the water, you bitch, but you didn't want to take it. You see Brenda, it's all about trust."

His words jar a memory for me, when Magnum spoke words similar to this. About building trust with each other. Magnum expressed the importance of the words, and not the silence in between them. I wonder if I can build up enough trust with David to at least get him to untie me. I have to try something if I want to stay alive.

"Yes, you're right. I'm so sorry for being silly. Can you please forgive me?"

He smiles and looks down at the floor. "Well, since you apologized. Yes, I forgive you."

I smile in return. "David, could you sit me up so I can get a drink of water too?"

He hesitates for a few seconds before helping me sit up. It's rather difficult, since my hands and feet are tied. He grabs the water from the floor and helps me take a sip. I say a quick prayer it's not poisoned, and I didn't just rush my death sentence.

He holds the back of my head as he helps me drink. He wipes my mouth with the bottom of his sleeve. "There, there, Bren. Don't drink too fast. We still have six more hours to go."

Six hours? What's going to happen in six hours? I blink, and my eyes suddenly focus on the digital clock sitting on top of the refrigerator. In six hours, it'll be midnight.

Midnight will be the anniversary of Curtis's master plan to kill me.

Chapter 30

<u>Fuckwithmeyouknowlgotit ~ Jay-Z feat. Rick Ross</u>

Magnum

Fucking accident on the highway made a forty-minute trip to the campground a two-hour one. Once we're able to get past the accident, I drive at breakneck speed to get to Brenda. Manny's been trying her phone, and nothing. Tick and Tony are on their way with some more backup, and I have no clue what the fuck I'm up against.

"Call her number again," I spit out angrily.

"Just tried. Will give it another try now." Manny dials her number again, then looks at me and shakes his head.

I bang my hand on the steering wheel. "Motherfucker. I swear, if he killed her, I will gut him with my bare hands."

"I'll help." Manny blows cigarette smoke furiously out the open window.

At this point, I don't argue with him about my no smoking rule. Honestly, if you can find a man who's willing to kill for your girl, he's earned carte blanche in my book.

I get off at the exit, and follow the GPS to the address. I drive past the house slowly as Manny scans the surroundings. The front door is boarded up with wood planks, and there's graffiti spray painted on the outside. Brenda wouldn't have gone inside this house. Besides, there's no sight of Cyma's car. I park several streets ahead and we walk back. We stare the small cabin for a moment before we look at each other.

"You sure she's here?" Manny whispers.

"This is the address that Cyma gave me." But he's right. The cabin looks empty, like no one has lived in it for years.

We walk towards the side window, and I peek through the broken pane. Nothing. No furniture or anything. It looks like teenagers and drifters come here to party and trash the place. There are empty beer cans and broken glass.

What the fuck? Manny is already dialing Cyma, and then it dawns on me. David is a dog owner; he comes here to walk his dog on the trails. I pull out my cell and search good trails to walk dogs in this area. Lucky for me, there are very few, and one stands out the most. It's the trail that's behind this house.

I tap Manny on his shoulder as he goes over the address again with Cyma. I point to the trail and he nods, quickly ending his call and following me. We both pull out our guns; there's no time to wait for Tony and Tick to get here. Silently, we walk up the trail a few hundred yards till we stumble on a cabin. We both nod, certain we have the right place. I signal for him to go around the back while I go to the front.

Manny runs around the back of the house and sends me a quick text message, letting me know he's in position. I edge my way to the front of the house and text him back. The door is old and gives way when I give it one forceful kick. It swings open, and I see Manny come in through the back.

Empty.

But this time, I know she was here because her cellphone is on the floor.

Shit!

Chapter 31
Dammit Man ~ Pitbull

Brenda

David drags me down another trail towards Kayuta Lake. His plan is to drown me, the way Curtis initially planned. Difference is, Curtis wanted to drown me in my bathtub on the day that he proposed to me and, well...this is not my bathtub.

Every time I try to scream, he hits me upside my head. The last hit, I think I saw stars. I decide not to fight him any further until we get to the lake. I won't be of any use to myself if I'm unconscious. Fin is running beside me, and if I didn't know any better, I think he looks concerned for me.

My back hurts as rocks and dirt scrape against me. Who knew a small man like David could drag me this far and not seem a bit out of breath? Occasionally, I look to my side and see the long drop to the lake. I close my eyes and say a silent prayer that I can figure out a way to get out of this. I manage to kick off a shoe and a few yards later, the other. Anything to help someone find me.

"What is that?" David stops momentarily, dropping my arms. I fall violently on my back.

I cry out in pain, but he doesn't pay attention to me.

Bending down, he grabs my hair. "Who did you tell?"

I try to make my expression blank. "I told you before that I didn't tell anyone. This is a hiking trail, and it's the season for it. Someone might be hiking right now."

I pray that my sense of logic works as he goes over what I said in his head. He seems to be happy about it, but then there's another sound, like a broken branch. Fin begins to bark, and David kicks him to shut him up. Fin lays by my side, whimpering.

"I'm going to check it out." With a menacing laugh, he adds, "Don't go anywhere." He turns and heads back in the direction we just came from.

This is it, my chance to get away, but my hands and feet are still bound. I roll to my side and move like a snake, but I don't get very far. I'm going to die out here in the middle of nowhere. Then I see a vision of Magnum coming before me, and I want to reach out to him; let him hold me one last time. That's all I want, and I could die happy in his arms.

But then my vision speaks. "Mooi."

I stare up at him, my mouth slack.

"I'm going to get you out of here." He bends, placing his gun beside him, and begins to untie me.

"You're really here?" I cry.

He stops and gives me a tender kiss.

He really *is* here. I'm not imagining this.

"Yes, now be still while I get these ropes untied." He begins to untie me as I concentrate on his features. He's here, he's really here. This is not a dream. Right? My head still feels foggy from the drugs and the hits I took but its undeniable that he isn't a vision.

"Where's Manny?"

"He had to turn back when a call from Tick and Tony came through. He should be on his way back now."

I close my eyes, thankful they're here. My hands are free and I grab Magnum as he kisses me.

"You came," I say, in between kisses.

"Always. Now let me untie your feet so we can get out of here." He pulls away from my reluctant arms and bends to untie my legs.

I'm so preoccupied with staring at him, I miss David, who has returned, and hits Magnum upside the head with a rock. Magnum collapses on top of me, the back of his head split open. I let out a bloodcurdling scream as David now rushes towards me holding the same rock he hit Magnum with. I reach my hand under Magnum and find his gun. Without hesitation, I lift and aim. David stops dead in his tracks.

A smirk appears on his face as if to say he knows I can't do it. Fin barks in between us, and I try to shut the noise out of my head as I try to concentrate. My hands begin to shake and tears fall down my cheeks.   He lifts the rock over his head and a hail of gunshots echoes throughout the vastness of space. A stricken look crosses his face before he collapses at Magnum's feet.

Magnum, bloody but otherwise okay, reaches over and checks David for a pulse, before glancing over at me and shaking his head. He'll need a few stitches and some rest, but it looks like he'll be fine. Fin is at my side and licking my face. While I know what David did was unforgivable, a part of me is torn at the loss of someone I once considered a friend.

Epilogue
Time To Pretend ~ MGMT

Brenda

I walk to the kitchen in my bare feet with Fin following behind me, trembling at the coldness of the Brazilian Cherry wood floors. Even though it's summer in upstate New York, there's still a chill in the air in the mornings.

Brrrr. God, I miss the city sometimes. But Magnum and I both decided to stay here for a while and heal. We're taking this time just for us, and I have to admit that I love it. His nightmares aren't as bad as they used to be. Now, he can't imagine sleeping in the bed without me, and I don't want to be without him either.

It's taking a lot of work on my part to not be as independent as I've become and I am learning to compromise more with him. It's a struggle from day to day, but I wouldn't change it for the world.

I open the fridge and start pulling out strawberries, whipped cream, Nutella, and a bottle of champagne, and start preparing breakfast. Occasionally, I drop a strawberry on the floor for Fin to eat.

I bend down to pat Fin, and he licks at my hand. "Okay, boy. Time for you to go outside while mommy and daddy have some alone time." I walk towards the back door and let Fin out to chase the rabbits or some other wildlife. He happily trots outside and runs around playfully, barking and yipping.

I go back to the kitchen and look at my handiwork, smiling. I load everything onto a serving tray and saunter back to the bedroom.

I nudge the door open with my hip and peek inside.

"Oh, damn. You're awake," I grumble as my heart drops. I turn and place the tray on the nightstand.

Already sitting up in bed, Magnum smiles, holding his arms open for me. I go to the man that I love and kiss him wildly. *How many hours has it been since I had his lips on mine?*

"Happy re-birthday," I say against his lips.

A few months ago, when he told me what his father did on his birthday that caused him to walk away from the madness of his house, I swore to him that his next birthday will be a re-birth of a new him. We won't fight those memories any more; we had a fucking funeral and buried it with his father.

"Thank you." His eyes are alight. He turns his head to look at the tray. "What's this?"

"A romantic breakfast in bed." Well, at least my version of one, since I really don't cook that much.

"You're spoiling your man, Mooi."

I nuzzle into his neck. "I love spoiling you." I pull away and place my hands on his shoulders. "I have another surprise for you."

He perks an eyebrow. "Mooi, I told you that my gift was you."

I stand up and slowly open my robe, letting the terrycloth material fall to the floor around my feet. Standing before him, I'm wearing a black leather bustier and a crotchless thong that I bought at Milly's Pleasure Emporium. My breasts are pushed up so high I fear if I sneeze, they'll smack me in the face. But I look fucking hot.

"Now that's the type of gift I'm talking about." He tries to rise from the bed in more ways than one, but I place a hand on his chest, stopping him with a *tsk tsk* noise.

"Not yet, I have *another* surprise for you." I'm more excited about this next one than anything else.

"More? Mooi, all I want is standing right in front of me."

"Magnum, trust me." I lay a feathery kiss on his lips.

Walking over to the dresser, I pull out a box with a huge red bow and carry it over to him. Milly and I searched for hours until we found the perfect set.

I place the box on his lap and bend down in front of him on the floor in the perfect slave pose Milly taught me.

"You don't have to do this."

"I want to do this. It's what I want," I profess, without lifting my head.

I hear the rustling of the paper inside of the box being removed and the opening of the inner box.

"Mooi? Are you sure? I told you I'm fine with the way things are with us. I don't want you to change."

"Magnum, I'm not changing. I realized that there is nothing wrong with this, and nothing wrong with me liking it. I want this to be a part of who we are."

Kneeling in front of me, he places his hand on me, and I rise to my knees, eye level with this magnificent creature that I'm lucky to have in my life.

Holding the gold bondage collar in his hands, he smiles. "Forever mine?"

Tears of joy fall down my cheeks, and I wipe them away. "Forever," I whisper, too choked up to speak louder. I lower my head as he places the collar around my neck and locks it. Before, I thought the sound of the lock clicking was me giving up all my control, but now I know that's not true. In this, I have more control, and it feels liberating. My heart beats only for him.

He holds out the key attached to a chain to me, which I place it around his neck. This is Magnum, in his own way, telling me the power is always in my hands.

Turning around, he reaches back inside the box and hands me the other collar I had made for him. My hands tremble with emotion as I unlock the metal clasp and recite the words he said to me moments go. "Forever mine?"

He stares deep into my eyes, grabbing my soul and uniting it with his, where it belongs. "Forever."

He bends his head, and I place the collar around his neck, locking it into place. I hand him the key on the chain, and he places it around my neck. Standing together, I walk towards the mirror, staring at my collar. I carefully trace my fingers over the metal and smile. Magnum stands behind me and holds me to his chest.

The bonds of our past have been broken by the bonds of the love we have for each other. Now, we are forever Bonded as one.

A Letter from the Author

Dear Reader,

Thank you for reading this book and taking this journey with me. You may be wondering how did this story come about. Magnum is based on a close friend of mine who was abused as a child by his father. His story touched me so deeply I wanted to put his words on paper and make others aware. As strong as he is he still struggles from day to day from the mental, verbal and physical abuse he suffered so many years ago. He is one of the most caring human beings I have ever met in my life, and he inspires me to be a better person in so many different ways. I am proud to be his friend, and I thank him for allowing me to tell a version of his story.

If you or a loved one were a victim, I beg you to speak to someone about it. If you know of a child being abused, please report it to the police.

For victims of child abuse, please call: Yes ICAN (888) 224-4226 www.yesican.org

All the best,

Autumn Sand

Reviews

I hope that you enjoyed Bonded. It would be great to hear from you, and I would welcome a review. Reviews are extremely helpful to authors. Your words help to guide me in my growth as a writer. Not sure of what to say? It could be something as simple as "I loved it."

Amazon: http://amzn.to/2qEz8u5

Goodreads: http://bit.ly/2qL7lGz

Acknowledgments

Thank you to all of my readers who took the time to read this book.

Now for the favorite part, acknowledgments. I could never thank these people enough who have helped me make this happen. First, I want to thank the reader for reading. I appreciate each and everyone one of you, thank you. Next, my incredible friend and P.A. Britta Neal who always manages to get me back on track. Jennifer Reynolds, my wonderful publicist, who is constantly promoting my work. Tracy Willoughby, Kelley Benson, and Natalia Schellhaas, who started out as readers but I now consider my friends.

Of course, I have to thank my street team, Autumn's Twisted Sisters! What an incredible group these ladies are. They are very supportive, and I love them to pieces.

As I get older, I learn, and I grow each day, but one thing I'll never grow out of is my need for my mom. My heart is full with thanks and appreciation for her and for standing behind me. Last but not least, I can't forget my cheering squad, Carl Kent from Powersmith Studios, Richard Rauch, Lucious Anderson and Melanie Cameron.

About the Author

Autumn Sand was born and raised in New York City. With her love of restaurants, her shoe fetish, and her hard-nosed heroines, Autumn is a New Yorker, through and through. Autumn has a shoe collection of 300, and the credit card statements to prove it. Other than shoe shopping, she has various interests, such as reading, writing, and traveling. Autumn has worked in the fashion industry for most of her adult life and recently decided to pursue her dream of writing sexy, thrilling, romantic suspense. She's reluctant to call herself an author but considers herself a person who writes words that people just so happen to like to read. Autumn has a sarcastic sense of humor and loves to make her friends laugh. She enjoys a good glass of wine, but her go-to drink of choice is a Jack and Coke with a twist of lime. None of those froufrou girlie drinks for her.

Autumn loves to hear from and interact with her readers.

Find her online!

Email: contact@autumnsandauthor.com

Facebook: https://www.facebook.com/autumn.sandsauthor

Twitter: https://twitter.com/autumn_sand

Goodreads: https://www.goodreads.com/autumn_sand_author

Website: http://www.autumnsandauthor.com/

www.ingramcontent.com/pod-product-compliance
Lightning Source LLC
Chambersburg PA
CBHW072229170626
46813CB00003B/1142